The Map of Marvels

David Calcutt

Other books by David Calcutt

Crowboy
Shadow Bringer

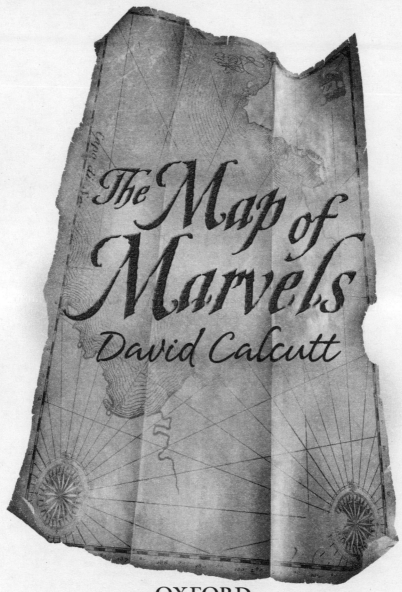

The Map of Marvels

David Calcutt

OXFORD

UNIVERSITY PRESS

OXFORD
UNIVERSITY PRESS
Great Clarendon Street, Oxford OX2 6DP

Oxford University Press is a department of the University of Oxford.
It furthers the University's objective of excellence in research, scholarship,
and education by publishing worldwide in

Oxford   New York

Auckland   Cape Town   Dar es Salaam   Hong Kong   Karachi
Kuala Lumpur   Madrid   Melbourne   Mexico City   Nairobi
New Delhi   Shanghai   Taipei   Toronto

With offices in

Argentina   Austria   Brazil   Chile   Czech Republic   France   Greece
Guatemala   Hungary   Italy   Japan   Poland   Portugal   Singapore
South Korea   Switzerland   Thailand   Turkey   Ukraine   Vietnam

Oxford is a registered trade mark of Oxford University Press
in the UK and in certain other countries

British Library Cataloguing in Publication Data

Data available

ISBN: 978-0-19-272967-5

1 3 5 7 9 10 8 6 4 2

Printed in Great Britain

Paper used in the production of this book is a natural,
recyclable product made from wood grown in sustainable forests.
The manufacturing process conforms to the environmental
regulations of the country of origin.

CONTENTS

ONE   The Map   1

TWO   The Ship   31

THREE   The Whale   63

FOUR   The Pilgrim   97

FIVE   The Desert   131

SIX   The City   165

SEVEN   The Tower   200

EIGHT   The New World   241

ONE
The Map

Connor was trying to draw a map.

On the dining table in front of him lay a large sheet of white paper. Next to the paper a pencil, freshly sharpened. A neat pile of curled shavings close by. Above the paper, a row of coloured pencils. He was all set and ready to go.

He stared at the paper. The paper stared back at him.

He was finding it difficult to get started.

'Come on,' he said. And then louder, again. 'Come on.'

Without taking his eyes from the paper, he picked up the pencil with his left hand and held it gripped between his thumb and forefinger. Then he lowered the pencil until its point was just above the clean, smooth, white surface of the paper.

'Right,' he said. 'Here goes.'

But the pencil stayed there just above the paper. His hand didn't move it any closer. He couldn't. He couldn't even make a single mark. He lifted the pencil away and stared again at the paper, and the

1

paper again stared back at him. Blank and empty. Just like his mind. Blank and empty. He let out a sigh of frustration and let the pencil fall onto the table and looked up and stared out of the window.

It was raining. It had been raining when he'd got up that morning. His mother had told him it would be raining all day. A steady, heavy, slanting rain that rattled against the glass of the window and spattered on the path and drummed and sploshed on the lawn on either side of the path. Just the day for getting on with jobs, his mother had said. So she was upstairs now gutting his room, and his dad was off at the tip because he was gutting the garage, and even his sister Alice was gutting her playbox, taking out all her toys and books one by one, laying them around her on the rug in the middle of the room. But Connor didn't have anything to clear out, or tidy up, or empty. He had this map to draw.

'You'll have all day to think of ideas,' his mother had said, before she'd gone upstairs.

But so far he hadn't had any ideas at all. His brain felt as wet and soggy and waterlogged as the garden outside. As grey and dark and heavy as the clouds from which all this rain was falling.

Perhaps the problem was that drawing the map wasn't his idea. He had to do it for a project at school. His English group were studying stories of travel and adventure, and for homework they'd been set the task of creating an imaginary world.

The idea was that they would draw a map of this world and then use it to write a story. Connor wasn't too keen on the writing part. He didn't really enjoy writing stories, nor reading them. Just a few minutes of writing or reading and his eyes watered and began to sting. But it wasn't like that with drawing. Drawing came easily to him. As soon as he put pencil to paper, it was as if someone flicked a switch inside his brain, and his imagination began to work. Like some highly-charged power flowing from some secret source down his arm and through his fingers and the pencil they held and out onto the paper. Sometimes he could almost feel his fingertips crackling with energy. Drawing made him feel alive.

But today, as soon as he'd laid the paper on the table, that power source had been switched off. Or maybe it was switched on, but there was some kind of blockage not letting it through. That's what it felt like. A blockage. And the more he tried to unblock it, the more blocked it felt. It was a horrible feeling. All that energy humming away inside him, and unable to get out. It was making him irritable.

And the weather outside was growing worse. The rain falling harder now, bouncing off the path, the morning darker, a wind springing up, flinging the rain against the window, tearing twigs and leaves off the large sycamore tree in next door's garden and hurling them onto the lawn. It looked as if there was a thunderstorm coming. Felt like it too. Connor's skin was starting to tingle, and there was a tightness winding itself round and round in the pit of his stomach.

He looked back at the paper. Still blank. Still no ideas. He picked up his pencil, held it lengthways between his fingers, then dropped it onto the table. It rattled. He picked it up and dropped it again. It rattled again. It was a good sound. He liked it. He did it again. And then again. Then he pushed the pencil so that it rolled across the table a little way then stopped.

'Connor.'

It was Alice. He spoke to her without turning round, dropping and rolling the pencil again.

'What?'

'You're making a noise.'

'I know. So what?'

'I don't like it.'

'Tough.'

'You're getting in the way. Stop it.'

'Getting in the way of what?'

He picked up the pencil, dropped it.

'My story.'

He picked up the pencil.

'What story?'

And dropped it again and turned round. Alice was sitting on the rug with her toys and books all around her in a heap of confusion. She'd made a small pile of some of them, toys and books together, and she was holding the pile steady with one hand while she placed another toy on top.

'I'm making a story,' she said.

Connor watched her. Alice was always making stories, telling them to herself, and to anyone else she could get to listen to her. Sometimes if Connor was in a good mood, he'd listen while she told one, but he could never keep it up for long. Her stories were long, rambling, strange affairs, with no real beginning or end, and most times not making any sense. Characters and events just seemed to jump in from nowhere, and then jump out again, making way for other characters and events which had no connection to those that had gone before. Listening to one of Alice's crazy stories, you had the feeling that it had started long before you'd begun to listen, and would go on long after you'd got fed up and gone away. All her stories were like one single, continuous story, that just went on and on and on, like some kind of long, meandering river, and you didn't know where it had come from, nor where it was going. Once, Connor had asked why her stories didn't make any sense.

'They do,' she'd said. 'They make lots of sense to themselves.'

Which in itself didn't make much sense.

Now he just said to her, 'Your stories are stupid.'

She glared at him.

'No, they're not!' she said.

5

'Yes, they are. Stupid. Like you.'

He was being mean and he knew it. He felt mean. Stretched and tight and twisted inside. It was that map and not being able to draw it. It made him want to be mean, and the only person in the room to be mean to was Alice. So he was.

'I'm not stupid!' said Alice. 'And my stories aren't stupid!'

Her face was flushed and her eyes were bright with anger. She was easy to wind up. He carried on doing it.

'Yes they are,' he said. 'They don't make any sense. And you don't make any sense. You're both a waste of space.'

Alice's eyes grew even brighter and wider. She wanted to say something horrible back to Connor but couldn't think of anything, so she squeezed her mouth tight shut and made a kind of grunting sound, and thumped the floor hard with her fists. The pile of toys and books she'd been building fell over. Connor laughed.

Then he stopped laughing.

A book fell out of the bookcase.

He didn't see it fall but he heard the thud as it hit the floor and he looked up. Alice turned to look as well.

Light flashed in the room, and thunder boomed outside, and the wind flung the rain hard against the window-glass.

The bookcase stood against the wall opposite the window. His dad had bought it as a flatpack from a superstore and had spent a whole afternoon putting it together. There were six shelves and it reached almost to the ceiling and all the shelves were filled with books: hardbacks, paperbacks, old books, new books, all of different heights and sizes and thicknesses. His dad was always buying books, mostly from second-hand shops, and there were so many of them now that they were packed and pressed tightly against each other on the shelves.

But now one of those closely packed books had fallen onto the floor. Connor could see the space on the top shelf where it had stood. And there was the book itself, a big, old book, lying a foot or so away from the bottom of the bookcase. As if it had not just fallen but had been pushed out with some force.

How had that happened? It was impossible. Connor looked at the book. Then he looked at his sister.

'Did you do that?'

'Me?'

'When you thumped the floor.'

Alice shook her head.

'I didn't hit it that hard.'

Lightning flashed again, followed by another thunderclap. Connor jumped.

'It's only thunder,' said Alice. 'There's no need to be scared.'

'I'm not scared,' said Connor.

'You jumped,' she said. Then, before Connor could say anything back to her, 'Perhaps it was the thunder that made the book fall off.'

'That's silly,' said Connor. 'Thunder couldn't do that.'

'Neither could me hitting the floor.'

Connor looked at the book again then stood and went across to where it lay and bent down and picked it up. As he did, he saw that one of the pages seemed to have come loose and was sticking out from the others. He opened the book to replace it and a piece of folded paper dropped out and fell onto the floor.

'What's that?' Alice was watching him.

'I don't know.'

He put the book down again and picked up the piece of paper. It was yellowed with age and had a dry, faintly sour smell, and it crackled softly beneath his fingertips as he ran them over its surface. His hands were trembling as he unfolded the paper to see what was on the inside.

It was some kind of drawing. Or a number of drawings. The lines faint and smudged in places and the paper itself creased and cracked and wrinkled, so that it was hard to tell what was a crease or wrinkle in the paper and what was a drawn line. Once, he'd looked at the palm of his father's hand and traced out the criss-cross patterns in the skin. What he was looking at now was a bit like that.

Just a confused pattern of random shapes that seemed to be scattered anyhow across the paper. He turned the paper round, this way and that, trying to find some shape that he could recognize and make sense of.

'Connor.'

It was Alice. He ignored her.

'This book's interesting.'

He glanced down. She'd taken the book that had fallen from the shelf and was sitting with it on the rug, turning over its pages.

'It's got stories in it. I think. And pictures.'

Connor didn't speak to her. If he did he'd just tell her to shut up. He didn't care about the book or any stories and pictures it might have in it. He wanted to work out what these faded drawings were. It was important. He looked at the paper again, and turned it one way and his head another. He squinted and drew it close to his face, then held it out at arm's length and opened his eyes wide and stared at it hard. He stared until his eyes hurt.

No good.

Too many creases and wrinkles. The lines too faint and faded. He began to get that twisted up feeling inside again, that tangled knot of tightness somewhere in the pit of his stomach. Just the same as when he'd been trying to start his own drawing of a map. He made ready to screw the paper up and fling it in a temper across the room.

And then it came to him. Suddenly he saw it. He knew what those smudged and faded shapes were. He knew what it was that was drawn on this wrinkled, yellowed piece of paper. And now that he knew it, he felt that he'd really known it all along, right from the moment he'd first seen it.

He laughed, and spoke aloud.

'It's a map.'

He sat at the table and placed the map next to the large sheet of white paper. The map was about half the size of the paper and curled up at the edges. He smoothed it as flat as he could with his hand, and it made a crackling sound, and he felt a tingle of electricity run through the skin of his palm.

Strange.

Strange too that just when his mind had been occupied with trying to draw a map, just such a map should literally fall at his feet. A map of some other world. That's what it looked like anyway. And it didn't matter to him now how strange it was. All that mattered was that he had a map now that he could draw. And he wouldn't have to think about it too much either.

Easy.

Outside it was raining heavily. The sky flashed, thunder rolled, and the wind whipped the rain against the glass. The room was dark with the shadow of the storm. He lowered his face and peered closely at the map. Then he stood up again and went to the wall and switched on the light.

'Why have you switched on the light?' said Alice.

'It's dark,' he said.

'It's dark in my story,' said Alice. She was moving her toys and books around. The book that had fallen off the shelf lay open beside her. She didn't look up at him and she had that concentrated look on her face.

'Well it's light now,' he said.

'Not in my story, it isn't,' she said.

Connor shook his head and went back to the table and sat down. He could see the map more easily now. Once more he smoothed it down. Once more his skin tingled. He flexed his fingers and picked up his pencil.

'Right,' he said. 'Now we're getting somewhere.'

Then he began to draw.

He began with the outline of a large island near the top of the map. It was roughly circular and had a smooth-edged coastline. On the map the edge of that coastline was very faint, but as soon as he began to copy it, making it clear and sharp on his paper, it seemed to grow clearer and sharper on the map as well. He put his pencil down and looked. Yes. The drawing of the island on the map had definitely become more distinct. He looked from there to his own drawing of the island. It was larger, because

11

his paper was larger, but apart from that it was an almost perfect copy. He felt pleased with himself, as if he'd done something right. He picked up his pencil and carried on drawing.

Next there was a large mass of land, a little further down, and jutting out from the right-hand edge of the map. It looked something like a strangely shaped hand, with clawed and crooked fingers reaching out towards the left. As if it was trying to grab hold of something. It gave him a shivery feeling. He felt shivery when he started to draw it as well, and somehow he knew that those crooked fingers of land were high, rocky cliffs pushing out into cold, grey, freezing seas. An icy wind howled in his head. Or was it wolves? Or both? He stopped drawing and closed his eyes for a moment and saw a vast wilderness of dark forests where wolves ran with burning yellow eyes and slavering jaws. Above the forests, craggy mountains lit by an icy moon.

He opened his eyes quickly and the vision was gone. But he had seen those forests and those mountains and those wolves. And even if they weren't shown on the map, he felt sure they were there somewhere, hidden. He'd put them on his own map later. For now, he just finished drawing the last, craggy claw of rock. And, as with the island, the outline of that rocky land on the original map had grown clearer.

He carried on drawing, and he drew more quickly

now, more easily, bent close to the paper, working with intense concentration. His imagination was fired and he was enjoying himself.

There was another large area of land at the bottom of the map. It had a long, smooth, undulating coastline, and as he drew it onto the paper he heard in his mind the hush of waves washing over sandy bays and beaches. But further inland it was desert, miles and miles of sand that glittered bright and hard under sheer blue skies and a fierce sun. And there, right in the middle of that desert, old and broken stones were scattered, half buried in the sand. Probably the ruins of some ancient city. Connor ran his tongue over his lips, and he realized that they were cracked and dry and his throat was dry too, just as if he was walking through that desert under that blazing sun. He could almost taste the sand in his mouth.

It was as if, as he drew it, that old map was coming back to life, appearing as it must have looked when it was first made. How long ago was that? Hundreds of years perhaps. Maybe even a thousand, or more. A map of the ancient world. That's why it looked so strange, so unlike any map he'd seen in a modern atlas. But how had such an ancient map come to be inside one of his father's books? Had it been hidden away between its pages when he bought it? Who'd put it there, and why?

All these thoughts and questions circled through

Connor's mind as he carried on drawing, with a fixed and intense urgency, hurrying to finish it.

He was drawing smaller islands now. There were many of them, scattered across the wide expanse of ocean that lay between the cold, snowy land of the north, and the burning desert land of the south. What had just looked like tiny smudges on the paper at first took on shape as he drew them.

But some of those smudges weren't islands. He looked closely at one and realized that it was in fact a tail. The tail of some large sea-creature pushed up out of the waves. Most likely a whale. He drew it on his own map, the narrow end of the tail lifting out of the water, the wide flukes spread and raised, looking as if they were about to smack down on the ocean's surface and send a great spray of water exploding into the air. And when he looked at another he realized that it was a ship, curved at the front and at the back, with a single square sail attached to a tall mast in the middle of the deck, and a smaller sail stretching from the mast to the front. Both sails were filled with wind, and the ship was plunging through the waves across the ocean. He felt a thrill of excitement as sharp and tangy as the spray of saltwater flung into his face.

The map really was coming to life. He was sure to get top marks for it.

He put his pencil down for a moment and sat back in the chair. His hand was aching, his fingers stiff, his eyes blurred and stinging. He rubbed them. How long had he been drawing? He looked at the clock on the wall. About fifteen minutes. Was that all? It felt like much longer.

He looked out of the window. It was even darker out there, a kind of purple, bruised light. The wind made waterspouts in the heavy, driving rain. The sky was a mass of bunched, black cloud. Thunder again, a crackle-spit of ragged light. The storm was coming closer.

He heard his mother upstairs, opening cupboards, pulling things out onto the floor.

The light in the room flickered. Then it went off. Then it came on again.

'What was that?'

The sound of Alice's voice made him start. He'd forgotten she was with him in the room. He wished she wasn't. He just wanted to be alone with his map. He didn't even turn round to face her when he answered.

'Nothing. Just the light.'

'Why did it go off?'

'I don't know.'

'It must have gone off for a reason.'

'Maybe it was to do with the storm.'

'Or it might have been magic.'

Alice's voice was very matter-of-fact. Connor shook his head.

'It was the storm,' he said. 'There's no such thing as magic.'

'That's what you think,' said Alice.

Connor didn't answer. He didn't want to get any further into that kind of conversation with his sister. He picked up his pencil and looked at the map he'd drawn. He was pleased with it so far, but all he'd actually drawn were the coastlines of the countries and the islands and the sea in between and around them. There was also the ship and the whale. What the map needed now were more details like those. That would make it really exciting. And he felt confident he could put them in. After all, he had seen, in his mind, what lay inside those countries and islands. The forests and mountains and savage wolves of the northern land. The burning deserts and ruined city of the southern land. He'd have no trouble drawing them into his map.

But for some reason he couldn't start. Something was stopping him. A kind of blockage. Just like when he'd been sitting at the table a little while ago staring at the empty paper. But now he wasn't staring at empty paper. He was staring at the island at the very top of the map. The one he'd drawn first. And the more he stared at it, the more he began to realize that it was this island that was the problem. When he tried to imagine what was on that island, there was nothing. His head was empty. Or filled with a kind of fog, a white mist.

The more he tried to imagine what was on the island, the thicker and deeper the mist grew.

What about the original? Maybe there was something there.

He looked, bending his face close to the paper. There, in the centre of the island, was a kind of darkish, faded ink-scratchmark. Or was it just a crease in the paper? No, he was sure it was something that had been drawn there. But it was so small and smudged it was impossible to work out what it was. And when he closed his eyes to try and imagine what it might be, there was just that slowly swirling, impenetrable white fog. He opened his eyes again, and stared at the inkmark on the map.

He had to know what it was. He had to be able to draw it on his map. Something made him feel certain. Without it he couldn't draw anything else. Without it the map wouldn't be complete.

But it was behind that swirling fog. A hidden, secret thing.

That twisted feeling was growing inside him again. A knot, being pulled tighter and tighter.

'Connor.'

He winced. His sister's voice was like a needle beneath his skin. What did she want now?

'Connor.'

He wasn't going to answer her. He had to concentrate, had to find out what that thing was on the island. He closed his eyes. Thick, white, swirling fog. But did he catch sight of something there, a shadowy form far back behind the folds of mist?

17

'Connor.'

Alice's voice cut right through his concentration.

'Connor, look.'

He gave up.

'What?'

'I've made something.'

'Good.'

'Look at what I've made, Connor.'

'I don't want to.'

'Go on.'

'No.'

'Please.'

'No.'

'Just turn round and look, Connor.'

'I'm busy.'

'Connor!'

'Shut up!'

'You've got to!'

'No, I haven't!'

'Yes, you have!'

'Alice!'

'Look!'

He swung round in his chair in a fury.

'What!'

She wasn't kneeling on the floor now, she was standing, and she had made a pile of her books and toys that reached almost as high as she was. Connor could see straight away that she hadn't planned it very well. She'd obviously just plonked one thing on top of another without considering the size or the shape or if it was any good for balancing or having things balanced on it. The whole structure was leaning a little, and the slightest tap would send it tumbling to the floor.

But Alice was standing next to it smiling.

'There it is,' she said.

'Great,' said Connor.

'It's finished.'

'Is it?'

'Yes.'

'What is it, then?'

'Can't you see?' She looked genuinely puzzled that he couldn't.

'No,' said Connor.

'It's a tower.'

'A tower.'

'Yes,' said Alice. 'A tower.'

There was a humming noise in the back of Connor's head, as if someone had just turned on some kind of electrical machine in there.

A tower.

'A tower!' he said aloud. 'Yes! That's what it is! It's a tower!'

Alice looked at him. 'I know,' she said. 'I made it.'

Connor swung back round to the table. The fog had cleared and he could see it now, standing there in the middle of the island. A tall stone tower. He began to draw it, two lines for the sides of the tower, wider at the bottom than at the top, and with curved lines at the top and bottom too, to show that the tower was round. He put in a door at the bottom. A heavy wooden door, which he knew was locked. No windows. Then he sketched rough lines up and across its surface, the outlines of the large, heavy blocks of stone from which the tower was built. Old, crumbling stone. The tower was ancient, it had stood there for centuries. And it contained a great secret. Something hidden away behind that locked door.

How did he know that?

He just knew it. Just as he knew that the tower, along with the secret it contained, was the most important thing in the map. Without the tower, the map would not be complete. Perhaps, without the tower, the map would not even exist.

He spoke aloud.

'It needs a name.'

And an answer came straight back.

'It's called the Tower of Truth.'

He jumped as if from an electric shock. He'd heard those words, spoken aloud just as he had done. He turned round to Alice.

'Did you say that?'

She looked up at him.

'Say what?'

'Did you say something?'

She shook her head. He knew she was telling the truth. The voice hadn't sounded like hers. But it hadn't been his own voice either. It had been some other, unknown voice speaking inside his head.

Or from inside the tower.

He looked at the tower Alice had made.

'What kind of tower is that?' he asked her.

'It's a magic tower,' she said.

'What's magic about it?'

Her eyes grew wide and she gazed into some place that wasn't in the room, or anywhere in this world at all, somewhere far off, the place where she was making her story.

'There's magic inside it,' she said, and her voice was very quiet, as if she was telling a secret. 'A big magic,' she said. 'And it makes lots of other magic things happen.'

'What kind of things?' he asked her. He was feeling pleased with himself and decided to take an interest in her story, at least for a little while.

But Alice didn't answer his question right away. She frowned, and then she said, 'I don't know yet. It's all foggy. I'll have to think.'

Strange that she should say that, when there'd been that fog in his head. But it was cleared now. He'd drawn the tower, the tower of truth, and now he could finish drawing the rest of the map.

There was a bright flash that lit the room for a moment, followed almost immediately by a long, racking crack of thunder that sounded as if the sky were being torn in two. Alice jumped and Connor

21

swung back round in his chair to face the window. The thunder had actually made the window-glass rattle. Rain was driving down in torrents so heavily from the massed stormclouds that it was almost like a sheet of solid falling water. He stared at it, fascinated. A little scared by it too. Then he glanced down at his map and saw the ship he had drawn there in the middle of the wide expanse of ocean. Imagine being on board that ship with such a storm raging all around you. Connor could almost feel the house rocking backwards and forwards, plunging through towering, crashing waves.

He was aware too that the humming noise was still inside his head.

'Connor.'

It was Alice again, standing beside him now.

'What is it now?'

She tugged at his arm.

'Look what's happened.'

'What?' he said.

She pulled at his arm again.

'Look.'

She was pointing behind him. He turned and looked. The pile of toys and books she had built lay fallen and scattered across the carpet.

'My tower fell down,' she said.

'Oh,' he said. 'How did that happen?'

'The storm did it.'

'No, it didn't,' said Connor.

'Yes, it did,' said Alice. 'It made me jump and I knocked into it and it fell over.'

'You'd better build it again,' he said.

She was looking at him.

'Connor,' she said. She was using that tone of voice, and he knew just what it meant.

'What?'

'Will you build it for me?'

'Can't you do it yourself?'

'I want you to do it. You're good at building towers.'

The window clattered and rattled. He glanced outside again. Sheets of water were being flung across the garden, and the wooden fence was being shaken and tugged, as if the wind was trying to pull it up out of the earth and fling it away. The storm sky was like a dark fist pressing down hard, trying to squash everything. Suddenly the whole garden jumped in a flash of white fire, as the lightning struck again, and there came another long splitting crack of thunder above the house.

And running beneath all this havoc of noise, that low humming deep inside his head.

Alice's fingers gripped his arm. She didn't seem too bothered by the storm. She just wanted her tower built again.

'Will you?' she said.

'All right, then,' said Connor, and he pushed his chair back and stood up.

He knelt down on the carpet among the scattered toys and books and gathered them together. Then he found the biggest of the books and laid it flat in the middle of the carpet. It was the old book that had fallen from the shelf, the one that had had the map in it. For a moment he thought about opening it and having a look at what it was about. But he wanted to build Alice's tower as quickly as possible so that he could go back to finishing his map. So he left it there unopened and began to place other books and toys on top, one by one, making sure he chose only those toys that were pretty regularly shaped—a small wooden drum, for example, a toy mobile phone, a large piece of jigsaw—and also placing them on top of each other in order of size; a smaller one on a larger one and so on up to the top. And all the time he was doing this, he could hear Alice talking, to him, to herself, to the whole room. To anyone or anything that was listening.

'The wind's howling—sssshhhhooooo—and the lightning's flashing—shhhtak!—and the thunder's booming—bangaboomabang! It's a terrible storm. It's so strong anything could happen. The wind might come and knock you down, and then pick you up, right off your feet, and carry you away, high in the air . . . whooooo . . . ' Her voice had taken on a sing-song tone, rising and falling, the secret, musical voice she spoke in when she told her stories. ' . . . far, far away to another country, and you might never come back again. And there's lots of magical things in that other country, and frightening things as well, monsters and giants, all kinds of horrible creatures . . . '

Connor had almost finished building the tower, and he was only half listening to what his sister was saying. But then she said something that made him stop, and her words cut clear through the noise of the storm outside.

'And here's a big tower made of old stone, and there's a door and it's opening, and there's a window at the top . . . '

What was that she was saying about the tower? And a window in the tower? He hadn't drawn a window.

' . . . and what's this face looking out . . . ?'

Suddenly she gave a sharp cry and at the same time Connor turned round and jumped to his feet.

'Alice,' he said, and there was a hard, brittle edge to his voice. 'Alice. What are you doing?'

Alice was standing by the table, and she was staring at his drawing of the map. When he spoke to her she looked up. Something fell from her hand and clattered and rolled across the table. Then the light flickered and went out and storm-dark flooded the room. But there was a dull, metallic glow that seemed to hang above and around the table, and around his sister's face.

And the humming in his head had grown a little louder.

'What is it?' he said. 'What's happened?'

He approached her and she drew back from the table. His heart was beating fast and there was a tight dryness in his throat. He looked down at the table, at the map he'd drawn. A series of thick, ugly pencil marks had been scrawled across the tower, deep and heavy lines that completely obliterated it. For a moment he couldn't breathe. He felt as winded and sick as if he'd been punched in the stomach. 'Why did you do this?' he said. His voice sounded ugly.

'There was a horrible face,' said Alice. 'Looking out of the window. It frightened me and I wanted to get rid of it.'

'I didn't draw a window,' said Connor. He could feel the anger rising inside him, like a lengthening, drawn-out howl.

'I did,' said Alice. 'I thought it needed a window so I drew one. And then there was that horrible face. But I didn't draw that. It was just there.'

'Liar!' he shouted, letting his anger slam outwards, making his sister jump and start back from him in fear. 'I spent ages drawing that! And now you've ruined it! You and your stupid stories!'

He was clenching his fists and his face burned. He felt as if he'd been flung into some huge machine which was grinding him up, tearing him to pieces, and all that was left of him was that terrible anger, and the need to lash out, strike at something, do some real damage.

'You ruined my tower!' he screamed. 'And now I'm going to ruin yours!'

And even though it was he himself who'd built it just a few moments ago, he turned and kicked out hard at the tower of toys and books. And as his foot made contact, and as the tower began to topple and fall, there came a cry from behind him, then a deafening crack, and something bright and sharp stabbed through the room, lighting it up. The floor shook beneath him and he lost his balance and stumbled sideways. Then there came a roaring, shrieking howl that whirled him round and thumped him on the back and knocked him down, then grabbed him and jerked him up again and lifted him off his feet, and the room was filled with wind and thunder and rain and he was taken and hurled right into the centre of it.

And then he was falling, tumbling and turning over as the rain and the wind screamed about him, dragging him round and down through a long tunnel of storm. Something smacked against his face and stuck there for a moment, then tore free again, and he saw it flapping away from him. It was the map, not the one he'd drawn, but the original, the one he'd found. He reached out for it but it went swirling and twisting and turning away into roaring darkness. That same roaring darkness into which he fell, and kept on falling.

Alice watched her brother kick at the tower. She didn't understand why he was so angry with her. She thought she'd made the tower he'd drawn look better with the window at the top. It hadn't seemed finished without it. But she hadn't drawn the face looking out of the window. It had just appeared there. And it had been such a horrible face, all twisted and ugly. Just like the face Connor had pulled when he'd been shouting at her. That had made her frightened as well. She'd never seen her brother look so horrible before. And it was because he'd become so horrible that he kicked out at her tower and knocked it over. But as he did the lightning flashed and the thunder cracked loud with a long rolling boom coming out of it and it made her jump again and cry out and she turned and looked out of the window at the storm. She watched the rain driving down and the wet leaves picked up and swirled by the wind and she heard the wind howling and booming through the creaking branches of the tree. Then she turned back and the light came back on and the tower was broken and Connor was gone.

* * *

He was falling, and falling, and falling. He thrashed out with his arms, trying to find something to hold on to. But there was nothing. Only the wind that clutched him as if with claws, dragging him round and down, and the rain that lashed against his face and poured into his open mouth so that he felt as if he was drowning. And the roaring, booming blackness all around him.

Then something struck him again, heavier and harder this time, and he was flipped over, and his head cracked against something solid, and he was sliding down it, and then falling through the air again, but only for a short while because a few seconds later he landed flat on his back with his breath knocked out of his body.

The storm was still raging, and he tried to stand up, but fell back again, because whatever he'd landed on was moving, swaying violently beneath him, and he went rolling across it, then hit something else and lay still. He was pressed against some kind of wooden wall, and he managed to take hold of it and drag himself up until he was standing at last, his hands gripping its edge. He could see nothing. The rain was lashing his face, and all ahead was pitch darkness, a darkness that seemed to be endlessly rolling and heaving, and it was all he could do to hang on and stop himself from being thrown from his feet again. Then he heard another sound above that of the screaming wind, a loud and heavy thump, again, and then again, as if some giant hand was striking at the darkness. Thump. Thwack. Thump. Thwack. It came from above, and he looked up, and gasped at what he saw.

It was a sail, bellied out by the wind, fixed to a tall mast that rose and fell with the violent swaying of the deck. Thick ropes danced about it. They sang in the storm, a deep groaning hum. Rain drove in torrents. Great waves piled up and came crashing down. The timbers squealed.

He was on board a ship in the open sea at night in the middle of a raging tempest.

TWO
The Ship

The ship was pitching and rolling, waves were battering it and crashing over it, the rain lashed the decks and the wind screamed. He could see little, though above him he could make out a glow of red light, which seemed to come from some kind of lantern tied to the mast, its dull flame swinging backwards and forwards, flickering and guttering in the darkness.

Connor was holding on to the mast, his arms wrapped around it, fingers locked. He was dazed and confused, and he had no time to think how he'd come to be on board the ship. All his thoughts, and all his energy, were taken up with holding on to that mast and making sure he wasn't torn away and hurled over the side into the ocean.

Suddenly there was a loud crack above him, and once again something smacked him in the face, so heavily that he lost his grip. He staggered backwards and his feet began to slide from under him, as seawater swirled and gushed around and over him, and he was tumbling across the upturned deck. He

31

gave a cry and flung himself forward, arms grabbing at the dark, at the wind, at the driving rain. Then the ship lurched and pitched and he fell once more against the mast. He gripped it and held on fast.

But that loud cracking, slapping sound was going on still above him, like the wings of some huge bird beating at the air. He looked up and saw that part of the sail had been torn free of the mast. Its ragged and tattered edge was flapping wildly in the shrieking wind, while at the same time a length of thick rope swung around it, and flicked and lashed outwards, and swung back, and flicked and lashed out again.

Connor pressed his face, his chest, his legs hard against the mast. He didn't know what else to do. All around him screaming, howling, tortured voices raved, and the storm stretched its jaws wide to swallow the world.

Then he heard another voice, sounding more human. It came from above and far off, as if calling out from the other side of the storm. Then it came closer, louder, swept past him, and away again. And then swept back past his ear, a long, wailing, human cry. Connor lifted his face from the mast and looked up, as the cry came unwinding towards him once more, and to his amazement he saw a figure go swinging past, legs kicking, cloak flapping, hands gripping the rope which a few moments before

Connor had seen lashing free and loose in the air.

And the voice cried out.

'Aaaaaahhhhh!'

It vanished into the dark, then came swinging back again, into the guttering flame-light of the lantern, with its cry flung out like another rope, invisible, a hopeless note of terror and despair.

'He-e-e-e-e-e-lp!'

Then it vanished once more into the whumping, piledriving storm darkness, and Connor wondered if this time both figure and cry would be torn away from the rope and thrown down that terrible, dark, howling throat. But no, here it came again, legs and cloak and hands and cry sweeping back, into the lantern-light, and those legs kicking frantically now, and a face glimpsed this time, twisted and wide-mouthed with terror.

What Connor did next he did without thinking. As the legs flew past he reached out and grabbed hold of a foot. The foot, and the leg, gave a jerk, the figure clinging to the top twisted round, and the other foot swung out and back and heeled Connor in the mouth. For a moment he felt himself being dragged across the deck, which rolled over and away from him, so that he was lifted into the air, and the cry above him became a high-pitched, half-strangled yelp. Then the ship rolled again, and he was dropped back onto the deck with his own legs running backwards towards the mast. He was still holding on to the foot and the twisting, writhing body above it, and when he was thrown against the mast, the figure above gave another cry and fell on top of him, and the two of them collapsed in a struggling tangle of limbs and rope and legs kicking and hands clawing and relentless heaving washes of seawater.

Connor pushed the weight off him and looked up. He was lying on his back, pressed against the mast, and there was a man's bearded face staring down at him, partly lit by the swinging glow of the lamp above, which threw arcs of shadow and red flamelight back and forth across it. The face and beard streamed with rain and sweat and the draggled ends of a soaked turban hung about his shoulders. The man shouted above the noise of the storm.

'Who are you?'

Connor didn't know what to say. Except perhaps to ask the man the same thing. But before he could say anything, the man's face disappeared, and Connor felt himself being pulled up onto his feet, and then he was staring once more into the man's face. The ship lurched and Connor stumbled forward against the man's chest and the man stumbled back too so that it seemed they were both about to fall over again. But before that could happen he was pulled back suddenly and felt a hand grip his arm from behind, and something cold and sharp pressed against his throat. And then a harsh voice spoke in his ear.

34

'Not one false move, stranger, or this knife of mine will slit your throat.'

Alice stood looking at the place where Connor had been. Her toys and books were scattered across the floor where he'd kicked them. But there was no Connor.

She looked round for him. Where was he? Was he hiding?

'Connor,' she said. 'Connor. Come out. I can see you.'

But she couldn't see him and he wasn't hiding. There was nowhere to hide in the living room. Except under the stairs. The stairs came down into the living room and there was a space underneath with the settee in front and sometimes Alice crawled into the space and sat there to read her books or play with her toys or tell her stories. It was very private and away from everywhere else. Like being in another world. Perhaps Connor was there. She went to the settee and looked behind it into the space. It was empty. He wasn't there. She came out again and stood in the middle of the room, looking around.

The storm was still going on outside but it was beginning to move away. The next thunderclap when it came was further off, and the house didn't shake.

Alice scratched her head and frowned. She was

annoyed that Connor had just gone off and left her. And broken her tower and left her toys and books in a mess. It made her angry when she thought of him doing that. She hadn't meant to scribble out his drawing of the tower. It was that horrible face looking at her out of the window. She'd just wanted to get rid of it.

Where had that face come from? How had it got inside the tower? She definitely hadn't put it there. It was as if it had been inside the tower all along, waiting for her to draw the window so it could look out.

She spoke aloud.

'It must be magic.'

Then she stood for a while, and then she spoke aloud again.

'A bad magic.'

She felt a tingle of thrill run through her when she said that. It was the same kind of tingle she felt when she was starting to make up a new story. Perhaps she was starting to make up a new story now. She went to the table and looked at the map Connor had drawn. Then she looked for the other map, the one he'd found in the old book. That's what he'd been copying. When she'd been drawing the window in the tower it had been there, lying beside Connor's map. But it wasn't there now. She wanted to look at that map. There might be something on it that Connor hadn't drawn, something that would help her make up her new story. She looked under the table to see if the map had fallen on the floor. It hadn't. She stood up.

It was strange. Connor had gone and the map had gone. Perhaps he'd taken the map with him. But where? Where was he?

She went back to the carpet and sat down amongst her books and toys. Maybe she should try and build her tower again. That might help her make up a new story. She had a strong feeling that building the tower would help her make up her story. She reached out and the first thing she laid her hands on was the old book. When Connor had kicked the tower over he'd somehow kicked the book open as well. There it lay, with one page a page of print, and the other page a large, brightly coloured picture. And as soon as she saw the picture she felt that thrilling tingle run through her, only much stronger now.

It was a picture of a ship in a storm at sea.

She bent her head to the page to look more closely at the picture, but then suddenly she froze, and then sat up straight and stared ahead, her eyes wide. And she sat there like that for some minutes, absolutely still. Listening. She was listening to something. As if a voice, some kind of voice, was talking to her, telling her something.

And then she smiled. She laughed. She clapped her hands together. She spoke aloud.

'That's a good idea.'

And then she looked again at the picture of the ship in the storm, and she was still listening because the voice was still speaking. And then smiled and spoke aloud again.

'Yes.'

And clapped her hands again.

'Pirates.'

Connor was terrified. The storm raged and tumbled about him, the wind screamed like demons. And those demons had the ship in their claws and were dragging it backwards and forwards, throwing it between them and catching it and throwing it again, and all the time screeching with demon-laughter. There was a demon's face lit by red flame staring down at him, and another demon was holding him with a sharp knife pressed against his throat. And that demon was hissing in his ear and he could feel the knifeblade beginning to slice through his skin.

He closed his eyes. The storm-demons howled with laughter. Then they picked up the ship and shook it violently and turned it upside down.

At least that was what it felt like.

He was flung sideways, and he cried out, and heard others cry out, and there was a sharp, sting-ing pain in the side of his neck, and then he fell and slid and rolled along the deck. He came to a stop when something fell on top of him. He tried to push whatever it was away but found himself tangled, trapped, some long, sinewy creature winding itself into knots around his arms and legs, squeezing, pulling itself tighter and tighter. He couldn't breathe, he was being strangled. It felt as if a giant snake was crushing him with its body. He kicked and thrashed in a panic and managed to struggle free of the creature and pushed himself up on to his knees. The coils that had held him slithered across the deck and were still. A coil of ropes, that was all. He dropped forward onto both hands, head hanging down, getting his breath back.

All this time the ship was still being tossed by the storm, and the wind was still howling, and waves were crashing over the sides. Through the noise he heard a voice cry out, the words lifting, then ripped away by the wind.

'Secure the sail or we'll be lost!'

And then fingers grabbed his hair and pulled his head up sharply, and he was looking into a face just a few inches from his own, the face of a girl, savage and fierce, glaring at him through the stormy dark. Something bright glinted close by and her voice hissed.

'I'm not done with you. Once we're free of this storm I'll finish the job and split your gizzard.'

She let go of his hair and was gone and he fell forward again. Then he twisted himself round to a sitting position, his back resting against something solid, his legs spread along the deck. He sat there, letting the heavy swaying of the ship rock him backwards and forwards. Further off, voices were calling out, the man's voice, the girl's, twists of sound in the wind, and the dark was booming and flapping and creaking, and the side of his neck was burning. He raised his fingers and touched it and gasped with pain and shock. There was a raw wound in the flesh there and when he brought his fingers away they were sticky with blood. The girl had cut him with her knife. She did mean to kill him.

He felt sick and faint. He wanted to escape. But there was nowhere to escape to. He looked up. The dark rolled, the mast swayed. A huge ghost-bat flapped its wings and the demons bounced and laughed in the rigging.

Then he was awake again. That was how he knew he had slept. Perhaps just for a few minutes, perhaps longer. Because now he was awake, though his eyes were still closed. And he knew that he had woken to the same horrible dream, and that it wasn't a dream because the ship was still swaying under him and he was still sitting on its deck, soaked through with rain and seawater. He could still hear the wind but it didn't seem so strong. And it wasn't raining. A little way off he heard voices. The girl's first, then the man's.

'It's passing. We're through the worst of it.'
'And still afloat.'

'It was a bad storm. I thought we were lost.'

'I nearly was lost.'

Footsteps approached, then stopped. They were standing over him. This time it was the man who spoke first.

'He seems to be unconscious.'

'We'll wake him.'

'Then what?'

'Kill him.'

'We ought to find out who he is, and how he got on board.'

'All right, Abbu. We'll do that. And then we'll kill him.'

'I don't know. He did save my life.'

The man's voice sounded friendly enough, but the girl's voice had that same fierceness and savagery he'd seen in that glimpse of her face in the dark. Connor kept his eyes shut, tried to look so deeply asleep that it would be impossible to wake him. But almost straightaway there was a sharp kick to his knee and he cried out and opened his eyes.

The man and the girl were standing on either side of him. There was a pale light and he could see more clearly. As well as the soaked and bedraggled turban wrapped loosely around his head, the man was wearing a kind of loose, long-sleeved tunic and baggy trousers that were tied at the ankles. The girl wore those same kind of baggy trousers and tunic, and her hair was tied back with a scarf knotted at

41

the side of her head. Both had sashes tied around their waists, and from the man's hung a sword with a wide, curved blade. The handle of the knife stuck up from the top of the girl's sash. Both were dark-haired, dark-eyed.

Connor looked from one to the other. He thought he saw a smile on the man's face. There was no smile on the girl's.

'Get up,' she said to him.

Connor pushed himself up to his feet. He found that he was standing at the side of the ship, with his back to the rail. That's what he'd been sitting against. Behind the man and the girl was a wide, high mast tied with a large sail. Another sail seemed to be stretched above the forward length of the deck. Both sails filled with wind, and the ropes that held them sang a deep booming note as the wind tugged at them. Beyond the far side of the ship he could see the lumped and churning water of the ocean, which heaved and fell and rose again in great, rolling swells. The sea, and the ship upon the sea, with its ropes and rigging and masts, glowed with a faint and flickering silver light. Connor looked up at the sky. It was still heavy with knots of dark cloud, but they were beginning to break, letting in here and there straggles of that same pale light.

It was dreamlike. But Connor felt the swaying of the deck beneath his feet, the tang of the spray flung against his face, and the sharp, stinging pain of the knife wound on his neck and he knew once and for all, that however unbelievable everything was, what was happening was no dream. It was real. Or felt real at least. And feeling real and being real amounted to the same thing.

Connor looked at the girl and the man. They seemed to be waiting for him to say something. But he didn't know what to say. So he just tried smiling. And the man did smile back. But the girl didn't.

'Who are you?' she said to him. 'And how did you get on board our ship?'

He tried to answer, to say something. But when he opened his mouth to speak no words came out, only a kind of half-croak, half-gasp. The fury of the storm still seemed to be raging inside his head, making everything a tangle of confusion. And with the turmoil going on inside him, and the ship rolling about and beneath him, he felt as if he was being picked up and hurled into the centre of the howling wind and rain once more. He reeled and began to fall.

The next thing he knew he was leaning over the side of the ship, gripping at the rail with his hands, staring down into the grey, rolling waves. Tears were streaming from his eyes, his stomach felt hollow, his throat was raw. He'd never been so miserable in all his life. If that savage girl were to cut his throat now he wouldn't care.

But then he heard the man's voice speaking beside him.

'I don't think this boy's going to tell us anything until he's rested and had some water.'

Then he was taken gently by the shoulders and led away from the side of the ship towards the mast at the centre. He leaned against the man, hardly able to walk. The man spoke again.

'In fact we could all do with some rest and some water.'

There was a small cabin there, fixed against the mast and facing towards the back of the ship. The man helped him to sit on the deck in front of the hut, then said something to the girl and stooped to enter the hut through a low, narrow doorway. Connor heard the sound of footsteps going down wooden steps, and then a few moments later the sound again coming back up, and the man stepped out of the hut carrying a small barrel and a long spoon with a large bowl and curved handle. All the time the man had been away the girl had stood a few feet away from him, glaring at him with her dark eyes, one hand resting on the handle of the knife in her sash. He'd glanced up at her once and tried hard not to again.

The man set the barrel down and levered off the wooden top. Then he ladled water out of it with the spoon and held it out to Connor. Connor took it and drank the water. It was cool and refreshing and soothed the rawness in his throat and did something to settle his poor, churned-up stomach. The man took a drink himself then handed the spoon to the girl.

'I'd better go and see to the tiller,' he said, and moved away towards the back of the ship. The girl took a drink of water, slurping it noisily from the bowl of the spoon. She never took her eyes off Connor as she drank, and never took her hand from the handle of her knife.

Connor looked away from her, out across the ship towards the sea and the sky. The wind had definitely eased a little, though it still blew strongly, and the waves no longer crashed over the ship onto the deck. In the sky the stormclouds were breaking up, bundled and hurried across the sky by the wind, and across a high, pale moon that cast its misty light on the ship, and on the waters of the ocean. Further off, a remaining dark knuckle of stormcloud, edged with flickers of white light. From its centre a jag of lightning struck downwards at the sealine.

He looked back to the girl. She still had her eyes fixed on him, and it was making him uncomfortable. Nervous. Even a little scared. That hand on her knife. He remembered its blade pressed against his throat, the cut across his neck. He could see her features more clearly now, and he realized that she was only about the same age as he was. But there was something so fierce about her, so wild. And the way she just kept staring at him. He wasn't going to let her make him look away again, though. And he wasn't going to just sit there in silence. So he risked speaking to her.

'Can I have some more water?'

He held out his hand, and by the look on her face and the way her fingers tightened about the knife-handle he thought she was going to attack him again. But she didn't. She gave him the spoon and he dipped it into the water and drank.

'Thanks,' he said. He held the spoon out to her for her to take it back but she made no move to, so he laid it on the deck beside the barrel.

He'd said something now, and he decided to say more.

'What's your name?'

'You're the stowaway,' she snapped at him. 'And I ask the questions. What's yours?'

At least she was speaking to him now.

'Connor,' he said.

She repeated it.

'Connor.'

And the way she spoke, it was as if she'd just eaten something that had left a bad taste in her mouth and spat it out.

'That's a stupid name,' she said. 'It's not a real name.'

The girl's mocking of his name made him forget his fear, and he snapped back at her.

'Yes, it is. It's my name. And it's not stupid.'

Her eyes flashed and she glared at him, and he

saw her body stiffen, and her knuckles tighten about the handle of the knife. Her mouth tightened too. But she didn't do anything. She just sat there, glaring. And he sat, glaring back at her. And they were both sitting glaring at each other when the man came back.

'I've secured the tiller,' he said. 'We'll keep a fixed course for the time being. Do you feel better now?'

The man was speaking to Connor, and Connor relaxed and looked up at the man. It was a relief to have an excuse to look away from the girl.

'Yes,' he said. 'Thanks.'

The man nodded and smiled. 'Good,' he said. 'Good.' He looked away for a moment, out towards the dark horizon. 'The sun will be rising soon,' he said. Connor followed the man's gaze with his own. The last stormcloud was gone now, and the sky was clear, filled with stars and the full moon. Edging the sealine was a faint glimmer of pale light.

The man spoke again.

'Are you hungry? I'm hungry. Shall we all have something to eat? Breakfast, yes? Yes.'

Without waiting for any reply he ducked into the cabin again and went down the steps, and a short time later came back carrying another barrel, smaller than the first. A sweet smell rose from it when he took off the top, and it was only then that Connor realized that he was hungry. The barrel was filled with dried fruit—dates, figs, apricots, raisins—very sweet, and very sticky. The three of them sat there, eating the dried fruit they'd scooped out with their hands, as the ship creaked, and the sails flapped, and the sky lightened above them.

Connor was so hungry that for a while he kept his head bent, pushing one piece of dried fruit after another into his mouth, letting the delicious sweetness fill his mouth and throat, and slide down into his stomach. He was so absorbed in the act of eating he seemed to forget for a moment where he was, and the strange and unnerving situation he was in. Then, when the edge had been taken off his hunger, he raised his head and looked up, and came face to face once more with the man and the girl, both with their eyes fixed on him. He stopped chewing, and swallowed.

'More water?' said the man.

Connor nodded. He picked up the spoon and dipped it into the water and drank. He swallowed again, hard. The man and the girl never took their eyes off him. And though the man continued to smile, the girl's face was set firm and fierce. As he laid the spoon down again he realized that his hand and fingers were trembling.

Something, he knew, was going to be required of him.

Without taking his eyes off Connor, the man spoke to the girl.

'What did you find out?'

And the girl replied, keeping her eyes on Connor. 'His name's Connor.'

'Connor,' said the man. And though he didn't say it with the same distaste as the girl had done, he did repeat the name a few times to himself, as if trying to get used to it. 'Connor. Connor. Connor. Hmm. Anything else?'

'That's all,' said the girl. 'For now.'

And the man, still smiling, still keeping those dark eyes of his fixed on Connor, leaned in towards him a little, and spoke.

'Well, Connor. Will you tell us now how you come to be on board our ship?'

Connor swallowed again. It lumped in his throat. His throat was dry, he wanted another drink, but he didn't dare take one. He tried to think how to begin telling the man what he wanted to know. But before he could, the girl was speaking.

'You ought to know that this man is none other than Al-Sindbaad Al-Bahri, known also as Sindbad, King of the Pirates, and I am Sherazhad, his daughter. We are the terrors of the Eastern Seas. Where we pass, the waves are red with blood, and all quake in terror at the mention of our names.'

And now at last she drew the knife from the sash around her waist, and raised its point towards him.

'Speak, and speak only the truth,' she said. 'If you lie we'll know it. And if you lie, a moment later I'll cut your throat.'

* * *

Connor told his story as best he could. It wasn't easy. He found when he came to try and think about all that had happened before finding himself on the ship, he couldn't seem to find all the pieces of it, or get them in the right order. It was as if his memory was some huge mirror that had been shattered into fragments by the storm and lay scattered all about him. In each fragment a different, broken part of his memory, unconnected to the others. So he said things like:

'The storm came in through the window.'

And:

'I found a map in a book.'

And:

'The book fell on the floor.'

And:

'I was drawing the map.'

And:

'I think I fell into it.'

When he said this, the man leaned forward again. There was puzzlement on his face, and in his voice when he spoke.

'You fell into it? What do you mean?'

'He's lying,' said the girl. She had laid the knife across her lap when Connor had begun his story. Now he saw her close her hand over it again.

'I'm not so sure,' said the man. 'Let's hear more about this.' He spoke to Connor. 'How did you fall in? And what did you fall into?'

'The map,' said Connor. 'The one I was drawing. Or the other one, the one I found. I don't know. And I don't know how.' He closed his eyes, trying hard to fit some of those splintered pieces of memory together. 'I was drawing the map. I'd nearly finished it. There was a storm going on outside. And then—'

He stopped. A piece of memory shone suddenly very clear and sharp and bright, so that for a moment it threw all the others into shadow. He looked at it and his stomach knotted. It was him kicking over his sister's tower, the books and toys flying through the room. There was his leg kicking forward, and there was his face, twisted unpleasantly, angry, vicious. It wasn't like his face at all, more like some kind of horrible mask that had been fitted over his face. He didn't want to look at it any more and opened his eyes quickly.

The man and the girl were looking at him, waiting for him to go on.

'And then?' the man said.

'And then,' said Connor, and he spoke in a rush now, 'and then the storm came in through the window and picked me up, and the next thing I knew I was falling out of the storm and I landed here.'

For a short while after he'd finished neither the man nor the girl said anything. The three of them sat on the deck in silence. Connor listened to the creaking of the ship. There was a grey, freckled light now, a paleness in the sky above. Connor shifted uneasily. He hoped the man and the girl wouldn't sense that he'd left something out. At last, the man spoke.

'Is this true?'

'Yes,' said Connor.

'You drew a map, and fell into it, here.'

'Yes. As far as I can remember.'

'A sorcerer!' said the girl suddenly, and she jumped to her feet. 'I said it was no ordinary storm. You remember, Abbu? I said it had the smell of sorcery about it.' She lifted her knife and began to jab at the air with it. 'And I was right. It was sorcery. And this is the sorcerer!' She stabbed forward, pointing the knife blade at Connor. 'He conjured the storm that took our crew and nearly sank our ship.' And now she raised the knife above her head, holding the blade aloft, and called out, her voice ringing across the ship. 'Death to him! Vengeance! Death to the sorcerer!'

Connor was stunned, terrified. Once again he was in real fear for his life. This wild pirate girl, whose name he couldn't remember, seemed intent on killing him. And the man, her father, whose name he couldn't remember either, wasn't going to stop her. Here she was, coming towards him, fury in her eyes, waving that knife. Connor did the only thing he could think of. He too leapt to his feet, and clenched his fists, and shouted in her face as loud as he could.

'No! I didn't make the storm happen! I just drew a map! That's all, that's all I did! I drew a map! You can't kill me for that! It's not fair!'

His body was shaking, his heart thumping, his face burned and he could feel hot tears stinging his eyes. He tried blinking them away but that made things worse. The tears welled up, blinding him, then spilled out and ran down his face. He was crying, and he couldn't stop himself, and right then he didn't care.

But his shouting seemed to have worked. The girl stood as if frozen, gaping at him, open-mouthed. And through the rush and drum of the blood in his ears, he heard the man speak.

'Sit down. Both of you. There'll be no killing.'

The girl lowered her arm. But she didn't sit. Neither did Connor. They stood, staring each other out. The man spoke again, more firmly.

'Sit down.'

They sat then, and the girl pushed the knife back into her sash, and Connor ran the back of his hand over his face to wipe away the tears. He sniffed.

'Good,' said the man. 'Now, I don't believe this boy is a sorcerer. He doesn't look like one, and—' He held up his hand as the girl opened her mouth to say something, 'he also saved my life.' The girl closed her mouth, and frowned. The man leaned forward and lowered his voice, as if afraid of someone, or something, overhearing him. 'But I think we maybe have sorcery here. That map you found, it seems to me, was no ordinary map. And the storm it brought, the storm that brought you here. As Sherazhad said, it was no ordinary storm.'

Connor shivered, although it was not cold. It was all that talk of sorcery, and the thought of the map, the map he'd placed on the table and drawn, of being somehow part of it. Even the cause of it. He remembered how it had seemed to come alive as he'd copied it onto the paper. How even the finding of it had been strange. The way the book in which it had been hidden had just fallen off the shelf by itself. As if it somehow had wanted him to find it. But what was that 'it'? The map itself? Or something else? He shook his head. Those tangles were forming again, tying themselves into knots. He wanted to clear them out of his mind. He wanted not to have to think for a while.

He spoke to the man. He remembered his name now. Sindbad.

'Will you tell me what happened?' he said. 'With the storm.'

'I will,' said Sindbad. 'Or rather Sherazhad will.' He frowned. 'The storm's made my memory a little shaky. Her thinking seems to be much clearer than mine.'

Sherazhad, yes, that was her name. And at her father's words, Sherazhad's eyes brightened, and she began speaking almost straight away.

'We were on the open sea,' she said, 'crossing the gulf between Arabia and Persia. It was a clear, bright day. The sky blue, not a cloud to be seen. A good day for sailing. The spray in our faces and the wind in our sails.' She smiled to herself at the memory of it, her voice growing gentle, and her face seeming to become gentler too. 'We were pleased with ourselves, my father, me, the whole crew. We'd eaten well and our bellies were full. And our hold was full too of the plunder we'd taken.'

Her father, Sindbad, stopped her there.

'Are you sure about that?' he said.

She turned to look at him.

'Of course I am, Abbu. You could hardly move down there for the rolls of silk and boxes of treasure. We'd been sailing up and down the Arabian coast for weeks.' A note of excitement came into her voice now, and some of that fierceness returned. 'Raiding towns and villages, sacking them, burning them, the houses in flames and the streets red with blood.' She shivered with the thrill of it, then turned to Sindbad again. 'You must remember, Abbu.'

There was a puzzled look on Sindbad's face.

'Yes,' he said, 'I must. I ought to. And I almost do. But . . . ' His voice trailed off and the furrows that ran across his brow deepened. He scratched at his beard, shook his head. Then he looked up sharply. 'There was no treasure in the hold when I went down there to fetch the water,' he said.

Sherazhad stared at him, and for a moment she looked puzzled too. Then she said, 'It was lost in the storm,' she said. 'Like the crew.'

'Ah,' said Sindbad. 'Yes. The storm.'

Sherazhad carried on with her story. And now her voice became fierce again, and there was that fierceness in her face, and her eyes flashed and she waved her arms wildly, as she told about the terrible storm.

'It came out of nowhere. All of a sudden there it was, a big black cloud of storm, right above us. And before we knew it, it had dropped down on top of us, and we were in the middle of it. Wind howling—ssssh-hhhooooo—lightning flashing—shhhtak!—thunder booming—bangaboombang! A terrible storm, a storm like a monster. And this monster had the ship in its claws, and it picked it up and shook it and threw it into the air. We turned over and over, and there were men screaming and falling out of the ship, and then down we fell again—crrraaash!—splaaaash!—and the monster opened its mouth and roared—ROOOAAARRR!—and demons came tumbling out of its throat and they took hold of the ship and pulled it this way and that way, and the waves were crashing over the ship—CRAAASSSH!—and the demons were screeching and screaming in the air.'

She stopped. Connor blinked. The sudden silence was a shock. While the girl had been speaking Connor had found himself back inside the storm, the ship heaving under him, waves washing over him, those demons screaming high up around the mast. Now all was quiet and still again, the air soft with light, the only sound the gentle creaking of the deck.

Sherazhad was breathless with the excitement of her story. Looking at her, Connor could see that she too had been living it again. But now her breathing grew calmer, and she turned to her father.

'That's what it was like, wasn't it, Abbu?'

Sindbad too seemed to be coming out of some kind of trance.

'Yes,' he said. 'Yes, it was . . . something like that anyway . . . ' He looked at Connor. 'It's all still a bit of a muddle. I do remember holding on to that rope though, and being swung about the ship. And you grabbing my legs and saving my life. And I'm in your debt for that.' He turned to Sherazhad. 'We both are.'

Sherazhad gave a tight smile. But she didn't say anything to Connor. Instead, she stood and looked up.

'The sun's rising,' she said. 'Let's go and watch it.'

She moved away from the cabin, and stepped round the mast and made her way forward.

'That's a good idea,' said Sindbad. 'And now that it's getting light we might be able to see just where we are.'

They both rose, and Connor followed Sindbad as they too stepped round the mast and went towards the front of the ship. It wasn't that easy. There was what looked like a second mast, but this one stuck out crosswise from the first and stretched across the deck towards the front, and then extended out from there above the sea. A sail was fitted to this as well, and to reach the front Connor had to weave his way through loops and coils of rope, and heavy wooden pulleys and spars. Some of these had been broken by the storm and hung loose, and the sail too flapped loose with ragged holes, and Connor tripped and stumbled his way forward, stooping low under the mast when he got there to stand on one side of it, because there was no room for him on the other side, where Sindbad and Sherazhad were standing together.

The girl was gazing out across the waves. Her face was lit, shining. She raised her hand and pointed.

'Look,' she said.

Directly ahead, out on the horizon, the sun was rising. The sky there was fringed and stippled red and purple and deep gold, and there were flecks of gold sparkling off the wavetops. Above, all was a deep blue. A few stars glimmered, pale, fading. The sun rose quickly, the morning grew warm. The flicks of light flashed and glittered more fiercely, and there was a deep, bright shimmer off the whole ocean. Connor's clothes, and the clothes of the others, began to steam in the heat.

'Well,' said Sindbad, 'here we are.'

'But where is here?' said Sherazhad. 'Is it our own world? Or is it some other?'

'It's certainly not mine,' said Connor.

They stood looking in silence for a few moments. The sun was rising very quickly, and its reflected light from the sea was a hard glare now that hurt Connor's eyes.

'It's very strange,' said Sindbad. 'There's something very strange about it all.'

Connor suddenly became aware of a stillness hanging over everything, the ship, the sea, the sky. He was filled with a sense of vast distances, empty spaces without border or boundary, this ocean and sky stretching endlessly away. His head reeled a little with it.

Then Sherazhad said, 'It's the sun.'

Connor shielded his eyes with his hands and looked at the sun. It had risen to a point where it stood now on almost a level with the top of the mast. Far more quickly than it should have done. But now it had stopped rising, stopped moving altogether. It hung there above them, a great bronze disc hammered into the sky, completely still. And the whole world beneath it completely still too.

Sherazhad spoke again, and Connor heard the gasp of fear in her voice.

'Look at the sea.'

It took him a moment or two to realize what it was that made her afraid. Then he saw it. There were no waves. The whole surface of the ocean, as far as the eye could see, was flat and motionless. As if he was looking at a painted ocean instead of a real one. Despite the now intense heat beating down on them from that stilled and riveted sun, Connor shivered, and his skin tightened with fear.

Now Sindbad spoke.

'There's no wind. Nothing's moving at all. Except the ship.'

The two sails hung limp from the masts. No flutter of air moved them. The ocean lay flat and still. No wrinkle of wave disturbed its surface. Yet the ship was moving steadily forward. Connor could hear the slow creak of its timbers, feel the rock and sway of its timbers beneath his feet. He leaned over and looked down. The water curled upwards on either side of the ship, a creamy white foam that lifted and folded back on itself. Further along the sides, the water churned and bubbled and frothed, as if something was causing a disturbance there beneath the surface.

Sindbad and Sherazhad had seen it too.

'Do you see that?' said Sindbad.

'I do,' said Sherazhad. 'But what is it?'

They moved further back along the rail and looked down. Connor ducked under the mast and joined them.

All along the side of the ship, from the prow to the stern, the water seemed to be boiling, casting up glints and flashes of greenish light. At first Connor thought it was just the movement of the ship making this disturbance but then he saw that it was something else. There were long, sinewy forms moving down there, a mass of them crowded together, their sleek bodies sliding over and around each other, writhing and twisting themselves into slithery knots. Connor heard the splashing sounds they made, the bump and scrape of their bodies against the ship's planking, saw the oily glow they gave off, making the water itself shine with a slimy light. The sight of them repulsed him, and he wanted to look away, but he couldn't, and continued to stare at them with horrible fascination.

'What are they?' he said.

'Snakes,' said Sherazhad. 'Sea-serpents.'

'Hundreds of them,' said Sindbad, then he straightened, and made his way to the other side of the ship, and looked over, and called out.

'They're here as well.'

Sherazhad and Connor continued to gaze at the sea-serpents below. And as he watched them more carefully, Connor realized that the serpents weren't simply writhing aimlessly in the water, they were moving slowly along the hull of the ship, from prow to stern, and then swimming back to the prow to begin the process again.

'Look,' he said to Sherazhad. 'Can you see what they're doing?'

'I can,' said Sherazhad.

Sindbad came to stand by them again. 'The same thing's happening on the other side,' he said.

Now they knew what was happening. The serpents, with their slow and purposeful writhing, and as if commanded by some unseen force, were making the ship move forward through the water.

'But why?' said Sherazhad.

'And where?' said Connor.

They all turned to look once more across the wide and motionless expanse of the sea.

'There's nothing out there,' said Sherazhad. 'Nowhere to go to.'

'Nowhere that we can see,' said Sindbad. 'Not yet.'

They stood, silent, watching.

And the ship moved on across that stilled and haunted ocean towards its unknown destination.

THREE
The Whale

Alice liked those slimy things. They made her shiver with horrible delight.

'Crawly, slimy things,' she said, and she made the fingers of both her hands wriggle and writhe in the air. 'Slimy snakes crawling across the slimy sea.'

She didn't know where they'd come from. Perhaps she'd thought of them herself, or perhaps it was The Voice that had made her think of them. It didn't matter much. Like it didn't matter much where The Voice came from and who was speaking it. It was helping her to make a good story, and that was all that mattered. And it was a good story. It had those pirates in it. She'd found their names in that old book. And it had those slimy snakes in it. And it had Connor in it as well. That was one of the best things about it, putting her brother in her story. Making all these strange things happen to him. Serve him right for being angry with her and kicking over her tower.

That hadn't been her idea though. The Voice had said she should do that. But it was a good idea. The Voice had some good ideas.

Once or twice she'd tried to imagine what The Voice was. Sometimes when it spoke it was close up, almost like her own voice when it spoke in her head, and then she thought that perhaps it was a girl, like her. But at other times it seemed to come from very far off, and then it wasn't like a girl's voice, or a boy's voice, or any human voice at all. More a kind of humming sound. Then it really was The Voice. With capital letters. The. Voice. Speaking to her, helping her to make up this story.

Now she was listening to it again. She sat on the carpet with her feet crossed and her hands clasped together and her head bowed. There was a frown of concentration on her face and she was very still. She was hearing what The Voice was telling her. Because it was time to put something else in the story. Those slimy sea-snake things were good, but the story wanted something better now, another idea, a bigger idea, something to come rising up from the bottom of the sea and make everything go crash. Something like the storm again but even bigger and better than the storm. This was what The Voice was telling her. Let's have something bigger and better coming up from the bottom of the sea, and Alice was saying back to it, Yes, let's.

But what was it going to be? Alice didn't know yet. It was down there somewhere. She could just about see it, far in the back of her head, a dark, shapeless shadow. What is it? she thought. And then she said it aloud.

'What is it? What is it?'

She was growing impatient.

Then The Voice was speaking again. And as it spoke the dark shadow began to rise up from the bottom of the sea and come closer in from the back of her head.

And closer.

Connor woke suddenly and found himself staring into darkness. Where was he? He couldn't remember. He tried to think but his thoughts were too jumbled to make any sense of. Then for a moment or two he thought he was in a cave, and there was an animal in the cave with him, growling. But the cave was moving, rocking gently from side to side. A cave couldn't move like that. And all at once it came back to him. He was on a ship, beneath the deck, in the hold. He'd gone down there to sleep, out of the hot sun. So the cave and the animal must have been a dream.

But the growling was still there. When he realized that his heart thumped and his skin tightened and tingled with fear. He listened. Not far away from him, in the dark of the hold, some kind of animal was making a low growling sound. The rasp and the buzz of it seemed to saw through the darkness and

Connor lay stiff and unmoving, wondering what kind of animal it was. What kind of savage creature might be crouching there in the hold of a ship? And why hadn't Sindbad or Sherazhad told him about it when he went down there to sleep?

Now that his eyes were getting used to the dark, he could make out dim shapes in the gloom, probably boxes and barrels. He remembered having to step over them and round them when he came down, because the hold itself was quite small, about half the size of his bedroom at home. There was a steep flight of steps leading down from the door in the cabin, and he could see them there, just a few feet away from him. Two narrow strips of bright light gleamed through the doorway at the top.

But between him and the steps lay the creature. He could see the bulked shape of it, hear the low rasp and wheeze of its growling. But it wasn't moving. Perhaps it was asleep. If it was asleep, perhaps he could crawl past it and get to the steps without it waking. He'd have to take the risk. So he eased himself up and round on to all fours and began to crawl slowly through the dark towards the creature. But he'd only gone a few paces when his hand knocked against something round and hard and it rolled away clattering across the wooden planking of the hold. At the same time he felt a sharp sting in his hand as if something had bitten him. He gave a yelp of pain and suddenly the creature leapt up before him with a snarl, and he cried out again, and tried to pull back, but a hand had him by the collar and there was a flash of steel in the dark and the point of a knife pressed against his throat. Sherazhad's face glared fiercely at him in the gloom and her voice hissed.

'What are you doing?'

He was so scared and shocked he could only stammer a few incoherent words.

'I was just . . . I heard . . . I thought . . . ' And then his voice dried up.

Sherazhad let go of his collar but she kept the knife point at his throat.

'You thought what?' she said.

'I heard something growling,' he said.

'Something growling?' said Sherazhad. 'Down here?' She took the knife away now and looked round. 'Where?' she said. 'What is it?'

'You,' said Connor. 'It was you snoring.'

Immediately the knife was back at his throat, those savage eyes stabbing at him with their own dark blades.

'I don't snore!' she said.

'I heard you.'

The knife point pressed a little harder into his throat.

'I don't snore,' said Sherazhad.

'All right,' said Connor. 'You don't snore. I must have been dreaming.'

She took the knife away.

'Right,' she said. 'Now get out and let me sleep.'

Connor tried to think of something to say back to her. Now that he was no longer scared he was angry. Angry with himself for being scared, and angry with the girl for speaking to him like she did. And putting the knife to his throat. Again. But nothing came to mind, and anyway he wanted to get out of that dark hold now. It was too small and stifling and the air was stale. He wanted to be in the light again. So he just gave a grunt and stood and eased his way round Sherazhad, and round some more boxes and crates, and then stumped heavily and noisily up the steps to the door at the top.

When he opened the door and stepped out into the cabin, and then out of the cabin on to the deck he flinched and shut his eyes from the shock of light and heat that burst suddenly upon him, and he stood there, blinking, and holding on to the side of the cabin, gasping. Close by, he heard Sindbad's voice.

'Did you sleep well?'

He squinted, and looked down, and saw the pirate captain sitting cross-legged in front of the cabin, smiling up at him. Connor tried a smile back.

'I think so,' he said. 'How long have I been down there?'

'That's hard to say,' said Sindbad. 'An hour. Two hours. Three hours. With the sun not moving it's hard to tell how much time is passing.' He took the lid off the water barrel and spooned up some water and held it out to Connor. 'Have a drink,' he said.

Connor drank the water, and then spooned himself some more and drank that. Then he handed the ladle back to Sindbad.

'Everything's still the same, then,' he said.

'Yes,' said Sindbad, and stood and arched his back and stretched his arms. 'No change. No anything. Except one thing.' He turned his head to the side and raised his face a little and sniffed at the air. 'I keep thinking I can smell land.'

'Land?' said Connor.

'Yes.' Sindbad frowned. 'Just every now and then. A little whiff of something that smells like . . . land. Yet there isn't any. Nothing out there but the sea.' He sniffed at the air again and shook his head. 'Strange,' he said. 'It's a strange world we're in.' He turned his head back and looked directly at Connor. He didn't smile. 'I'd like to know more about the map you said you drew.'

'So would I.'

It was Sherazhad, standing in the doorway behind Connor. She pushed past him and picked up the ladle and thrust it into the water, bringing it quickly to her mouth, gulping the water down. She looked at Connor then as she filled the ladle again.

'After you woke me I couldn't get back to sleep,' she said, and took another drink, and wiped her hand across her mouth. She dropped the ladle by the side of the barrel and grinned at her father. 'He thought I was a wild animal, Abbu,' she said. 'Growling in the dark.' She pulled a face and made a growling sound and laughed.

'You are,' said Sindbad.

Sherazhad stopped laughing and stared at her father.

'No, I'm not,' she said.

Sindbad stared back at her.

'You can be very frightening,' he said.

And then he grinned, and she grinned too.

'I know,' she said. Then she turned back to Connor. 'Right,' she said to him. 'What about this map?'

Connor was really beginning to be irritated by the way the girl spoke to him. He wouldn't have taken it from anyone at home. He'd have stood up to them, given back as good as he got. And more. But he wasn't at home. He was here, in this strange world, lost, and confused. And the girl had a knife. The cut on his neck still smarted. So he just said to her, 'What about it?'

'What did it look like?'

Connor thought. He could see the map clearly in his head, could see himself sitting at the table drawing it, his hand moving the pencil across the paper. He could feel the hardness of the pencil between his fingers and thumb, hear the soft scraping sound it made as he drew the outline of the countries on the map. And those outlines, and the shapes of those countries were sharp and precise in every detail. Yes, he could see the map, but could he describe it? Could he make that picture as real with words as it was now in his mind? He couldn't, and he knew it, and he shook his head.

'It would be easier if I could draw it,' he said.

'Then draw it,' said Sindbad.

'I can't. I haven't got anything to draw with. Or on.'

'There might be something in the hold. Some old charts. And perhaps something to draw with.' Sindbad spoke to Sherazhad. 'Will you go and look?'

A brief look of indignation flashed across her face and for a moment Connor thought she was going to refuse. But the moment and the look passed, and Sherazhad bowed her head and said, 'Of course, Abbu,' and went into the cabin.

'Leave the door open,' said Sindbad. 'It should give you enough light to see by down there.'

Sherazhad went down the steps, leaving the door open behind her.

While they waited, Sindbad took a drink of water from the barrel, then stepped away from the cabin onto the deck. He looked up at the mast, shading his eyes with his hand. He took his hand away and looked down.

'Still no wind,' he said. He looked out across the sea. 'No movement anywhere, except for us.' And he stood, hands clasped behind his back, gazing thoughtfully into the vast, stilled distance.

Connor too stepped away from the cabin and looked at Sindbad, studying him. In the bright sunlight the man seemed to shine with an intensity that was somehow more than real. The vivid red of his tunic, the deep green of his turban, the curve and glint of the broad-bladed sword that hung from his side. To Connor's eyes he seemed for that moment as stilled and motionless and strange as the waveless ocean, the stopped sun. The ship too on which he was standing. Strange, all strange, unknown and unfamiliar. And suddenly he was aware of himself in the midst of that strangeness, and all about him shimmering with such a burnished, polished light as if on the point of misting and dissolving, and himself falling once more into some dark and storm-howled tunnel.

He must have made a sound, of panic, or fright, because Sindbad turned to him and spoke.

'Are you all right?'

And the voice was real. The face looking at him, its tanned, sun-wrinkled skin, the dark beard freckled with red and specks of grey, that was real. The whole man a real man. About the same age as his dad. A loose strand of turban suddenly unwound itself and flopped down over his eyes. He lifted it up and grinned.

'It keeps doing that,' he said. 'The storm ruined it. I don't know why I'm keeping it on.'

And he took the loose strand and unwound the turban into a single length of cloth and let it drop on the deck. His dark, wavy hair hung down about his ears.

'That's better,' he said.

And Connor too felt better again. He took a couple of steps towards Sindbad.

'Can I ask you something?' he said.

'Of course,' said Sindbad.

'Your name's Sindbad, isn't it?'

'Yes.'

'But Sherazhad keeps calling you Abbu. Is that, like, short for Sindbad, or something?'

Sindbad gave a laugh.

'No,' he said, 'Abbu means father. I'm her father, so she calls me Abbu.'

'Oh, right,' said Connor.

'Though to tell you the truth . . . ' Sindbad hesitated, as if he wasn't sure that he should carry on with what he was going to say. But he did. 'To tell you the truth, I don't feel like her father. I don't feel she's my daughter. But she's so certain of it. She's so certain of everything. And I don't really dare to say anything to her about it. She's quite fierce, isn't she?'

'She is,' said Connor.

Sindbad smiled, then that hesitant, puzzled look came to his face again.

'I'm not certain of anything. Not since the storm. All I know for sure is that my name is Sindbad, and this is my ship.' Then he turned and gazed out once more towards the hammered blue of the sky, the hard, metal glitter of the unmoving sea. And there was a darkness in his voice when he spoke. 'And this is not my world, nor any other's.'

There was movement on the deck behind him. Sherazhad came walking towards them from the cabin. In one hand was a piece of paper. In the other an oval shaped bottle of red clay. She held the paper out to Connor. 'I found this,' she said. 'It was in an old book.' She looked at Sindbad. 'The pages were full of writing, except for this one, at the end. I tore it out.' Then to Connor again. 'You can draw on that.'

Connor took the paper. It was a bit bigger than a page from one of his school exercise books, and it was creased and stained and one edge ragged where it had been torn out.

'What was the writing in the book?' Sindbad asked Sherazhad.

'I don't know,' she said. 'I can't read, can I? Pirates don't have time to learn to read.' She held up the bottle. 'Look, I found this too.' The surface of the bottle was covered with geometric shapes—squares and triangles of different sizes, crosses, zigzags, all cut haphazardly into the clay. 'It was rolling loose on the floor. And it seemed to burn me when I picked it up. But it's all right now.'

Connor remembered the round object he'd

knocked against when he'd been down there, the sharp sting in his hand.

'Let me see,' said Sindbad, and held his hand out. Sherazhad gave him the bottle. He turned it round in his hands, looking at the patterns on its surface. 'Curious,' he said. 'Very curious. I wonder what's inside?'

'I tried to see,' said Sherazhad, 'but I couldn't get the stopper out.'

'I'll try,' said Sindbad, and he took hold of the stopper in the bottle's neck and began to twist it.

Both Sindbad and the girl seemed to have forgotten about the map.

'Didn't you find anything to draw with?' Connor asked Sherazhad.

'No,' said Sherazhad, then turned back to Sindbad. 'It's pushed in tight,' she said to him.

Sindbad was straining as he tried to twist the stopper round, his mouth set, his knuckles whitening with the effort.

'You're right,' he said, and gasped, and let go of the stopper.

Suddenly a thought came to Connor. He put his hand in his jeans pocket. Nothing. Then he tried the other one. Yes. It was there. A piece of broken pencil. He must have put it in his pocket after he'd finished drawing the map, though he couldn't remember doing it.

Sindbad took hold of the stopper again and made another effort to twist it loose.

'It's stuck fast,' said Sherazhad.

Connor took the piece of broken pencil out of his pocket.

'Look,' he said.

Sindbad was still straining at the stopper.

'What?' he said.

'A pencil.'

'What?' said Sherazhad. She peered at the broken stub lying on his palm.

'A pencil,' said Connor. 'I can draw with this.' He shrugged. 'If you still want to know about the map.'

'Of course we do,' said Sindbad, and let go of the stopper once more. 'That's the most important thing. The map.' He handed the bottle back to Sherazhad. 'We can try this again later.'

Sherazhad took the bottle, and while Connor was sitting himself down on the deck, and smoothing out the paper in front of him, she undid the sash at her waist and folded it to half its width, then wound it around the neck of the bottle and pulled it tight. Then she tied the sash around her waist again so that the bottle hung there at her side. Then she too sat down. By this time Connor was ready to begin.

He sat with the paper before him, the pencil stub in his hand. The pencil must have broken during the storm. The other half hadn't been in his pocket though. He didn't know what had happened to that. Luckily this was the half with the point. A bit blunt but it would be all right. He blinked his eyes, shook his head. Why was he thinking about that? Why was he thinking about the pencil? It didn't matter about the pencil. What mattered was drawing the map. He blinked again, then wiped the sweat away from his eyes with finger and thumb. He was hot. His face, the top of his head were burning.

'Are you going to start?'

It was Sherazhad, sitting to his right. Sindbad was sitting to his left. They were waiting for him.

'Yes,' he said, and he leaned forward. But he didn't start. And he knew why. He knew what it was. He was afraid. Afraid that once he started drawing the map it would happen again. The magic, or whatever it was. And if it did, wouldn't that mean he was the cause of it?

'Go on, then,' said Sherazhad.

Her voice was sharp. It jolted Connor. Of course he wasn't the cause of the magic. If there was any magic it was in the other map, the one he'd found. This was just a tatty piece of paper torn out of a book, and he was just an ordinary boy, about to draw on it. Still, to be on the safe side, he wouldn't put everything in that he remembered. He'd just make a quick sketch.

So he put the pencil to the paper and started to draw, quick, rough lines, talking at the same time.

'There was an island here, right at the top, and it looked something like this . . . '

But no sooner had he started, than Sindbad said, 'Wait.'

He looked up. Sindbad was sitting upright, stiff, alert, his face raised.

'I can smell land again,' he said. 'And it's stronger now.'

And now Connor could smell it too, the sudden, rich deep scent of earth and grass, passing on the breeze.

The breeze! He felt it brush across his face. Sherazhad felt it at the same time.

'The air's moving,' she said. Then she looked up. 'And the sail.'

They all stood quickly. Above them, the sail lifted gently away from the mast, and a ripple ran all along its edge, and fell and lifted again, like the slow-flapping wing of some great bird.

They stood gazing up at it for a moment, then all three ran to the ship's side and looked out.

There was the deep blue sky, the ocean spreading to the horizon. But high up in the sky a wisp of cloud drifted. And the ocean's surface glittered and flashed with the sun's light on its waves.

'Look there.'

It was Sindbad, pointing down to the water beneath them. The serpents which had been swarming about the hull were moving away from it now, leaving the ship, their long bodies writhing through the water, diving beneath it, deeper, and deeper, until they were gone from sight.

The breeze lifted, blowing stronger. The sail ruffled, slapped, boomed.

The ship sped on across the waves.

The sea, the wind, the sun, were moving again.

And it had happened when Connor had started to draw the map.

Once more Connor sat on the deck with the paper laid out before him, Sherazhad and Sindbad sitting on either side of him. But now the heat was not quite so concentrated or intense, tempered as it was by the wind that billowed the sails and drove the ship across the thumping waves. The deck swayed and creaked. A little way off, there was the raucous, rasping cry of gulls. The birds had appeared shortly after they'd seen the sea-serpents swim away. Almost as if from nowhere. One moment the sky was empty, the next there were seven or eight large gulls circling and diving and skreeking with their hard and quarrelsome voices in the air above and around the ship.

'We must be near land,' Sindbad had said, and scratched his head, baffled. 'But there's none in sight.'

Connor and Sherazhad had scanned the horizon from both sides of the ship, from the prow and from the stern. Sindbad had climbed the mast and clung to the top, looking out. But none of them had been able to see any sign of land.

So they had sat and Connor had taken up his drawing of the map. His sketching of it at least. He was still nervous about what might happen if he drew the whole thing in detail. It would seem that even just putting pencil to paper had brought about some change, and quite a significant one at that. Now the wind blew, and the sun was moving across the sky, and the ocean swelled and dipped about them. And the sea-serpents had gone, as mysteriously as they had appeared. Had his simple drawing of a line on the paper done that?

He sketched the outlines of the map quickly, then sat back.

'It was something like that,' he said.

Sindbad and Sherazhad studied what he'd drawn.

'There's not much there,' said Sherazhad. 'What about this big empty space in the middle?'

'That's the sea,' said Connor.

'That must be where we are now,' said Sindbad. 'If this is a map of the world we're in.'

'Isn't there anything else there?' said Sherazhad.

Connor knew he was going to have to tell them about the tower. The Tower of Truth. That was the most important thing on the map, he knew that. But he wanted to delay it as long as he could.

'There were a few islands,' he said, 'but I can't remember exactly where they were. Nor the ship.'

Sherazhad stared at him.

'The ship? There was a ship? You drew a ship?'

Connor nodded.

Sherazhad spoke to Sindbad. 'He drew a ship!' And to Connor again. 'You drew a ship! Our ship!' Her eyes blazed with fury again and her hand went to her knife. 'So it was you who brought us here!'

'If I did I didn't mean to!' Connor said to her.

'Sorcerer!'

'No I'm not. I didn't mean to bring myself here either. It just happened.'

Sindbad reached across and laid his hand gently, firmly on Sherazhad's arm.

'Connor is telling the truth,' he said. 'And you know he is.'

For a moment or two they remained fixed like that, Sindbad with his hand on the girl's arm, the girl still with her hand gripping the handle of the knife, that feral light burning in her eyes. Then she took her hand away from the knife, and her shoulders dropped a little, and she looked away to the side. Sindbad took his hand away then and spoke to Connor.

'Why did you draw a ship?'

'It was on the other map. The one I was copying, the one I found in the book.'

'What else did you draw?' said Sindbad.

Connor sat thinking. Then he remembered.

'There was a whale,' he said. 'Something like a whale, anyway. A big tail sticking up out of the water.'

'Was it near the ship?'

'Not very near, I don't think.'

Sindbad nodded.

'And anything else?'

And now Connor knew he would have to tell them.

'There's a tower,' he said.

Instantly, Sindbad was alert, though he himself couldn't have said why. Sherazhad too sat upright again, fixed her eyes on him.

'What kind of tower?' said Sindbad.

He told them. Described it. Said where it stood. Named it.

'It's called the Tower of Truth.'

As he said them, the words seemed to crackle in the air, and the air grew taut, stretched, about the ship. And beneath the sound of the wind in the sail, and of the waves slapping the sides of the ship, and of the gulls crying as they wheeled above the mast, he heard the sound of a deep, far-off, low humming.

The words had an effect on Sindbad and Sherazhad too. He could see it in their suddenly alert faces, hear it in their tensed voices.

'The Tower of Truth,' said Sindbad.

'Yes,' said Connor.

'Where is it?' said Sherazhad.

Connor pointed to the island he'd sketched at the top of the paper.

'Here,' he said.

'The Tower of Truth,' Sindbad said again. 'It sounds important.'

'I think it is,' said Connor.

'Was the name written on the map?'

'No. It just came to me, after I'd drawn it.' He remembered how it had sounded as if some other voice had spoken the words. But he didn't tell them that. 'I know that's what it's called,' he said.

'Draw it,' said Sherazhad.

He knew there was no avoiding it now. He'd have to draw it. But he was still reluctant to. He was beginning to think it was the tower that was somehow behind all that was happening. He thought of Alice scribbling over the tower on his map. Of himself kicking over her tower of books and toys. That was when the storm had come that had brought him here, and had brought the pirate captain and his daughter here too in their ship. If he drew the tower again now, would something else happen, equally strange? Or even stranger?

'Draw it,' said Sherazhad again.

Connor placed the tip of the pencil on the paper, in the middle of the island. But before he could make a single mark, a sudden gust of wind swept across the deck, snatched the paper from beneath his hand and lifted it into the air and carried it away towards the side of the ship. And there it stuck, fluttering as if held flat against it by one invisible hand,

and another tugging and twisting at its upper edge, trying to pull it free and fling it into the waves.

Connor gave a cry as the paper flew away from him, and straight away was on his feet and running to the side of the ship to take hold of the paper before it did fly away. And he almost made it. But just as he was within reach, and stretching out his hand towards it, a harsh and raucous scream ripped through the air above him, and a large gull swooped down past him, so close that he felt the tip of its wing scrape the side of his face, and it grabbed the paper in its beak and flew up with it away from the ship and above the sea.

'No!' Connor cried out again. 'What is it? What's going on?'

Because it was all just too much of a coincidence that all this should happen just as he was about to draw the Tower. As if something, some hidden, secret force, was determined that he should not draw it, and was summoning up all its hidden, secret powers to make sure that he didn't. He stood there, staring up at the gull that wheeled and turned high above the waves with the paper in its beak, and although he knew it wouldn't do any good, he started shouting up at the gull. Sindbad and Sherazhad joined him, and they were shouting at it as well. Sherazhad climbed up and stood on the side of the ship waving her knife in the air, and Connor thought for a moment she was going to throw it and try and bring the bird down. And perhaps she might have done if a sudden screech from above hadn't startled her, and made her lose her balance and tumble backwards on to the deck.

The screeching came from two more gulls that came divebombing down from the mast straight towards the first gull, coming in at it from either side. The first gull twisted itself round in the air and swerved out of the flightpath of the other birds and plunged towards the sea. It flew sideways for a few moments so that the tip of the downturned wing actually skimmed along the wavetops, then righted itself and swept in a long curve up into the air again. All the time it had the paper clapped firmly in its beak.

But the two attacking gulls themselves swept upwards after the first and soon were mobbing it again, one from below and one from above, beating at it with their wings and striking at it with their beaks, and though the first swerved and turned and twisted its body away it could not escape them. At last one of the two flew high above the mast and gave a long, rag-edged scream and dived down along the track of that scream straight at the first gull. Then the harried bird staggered in its flight and whipped itself up and round, and let out a screech of rage and the paper fell from its beak and swirled round and floated down to come to rest on the surface of the sea, not far from the ship.

And with that the gulls stopped their fighting, and all three sailed down towards the mast and perched there, one on top of the mast, the other two on either end of the crossbeam.

'Lower the sail!' cried Sindbad. 'We have to stop the ship.'

'Why?' said Connor.

'We'll leave the map behind,' he said.

And straight away he and Sherazhad ran to the ropes that held the sail in place and unlashed them, and lowered the sail on its crossbeam. The two gulls that had just perched there yapped and squawked in annoyance, and flapped down to perch on the prow. The first remained atop the mast, flapping its wings like some large, grey flag. Then Sindbad and Sherazhad loosened the ropes that held the smaller sail in place and lowered that too. The two gulls perched on the prow watched them with their wild and gold-bright eyes.

With the sails down the ship slowed, and soon came to rest. And Sindbad and Sherazhad had worked so quickly, and so expertly, that, although they had moved some distance from the paper, it was still visible. In fact, it seemed to be moving closer.

'There's a current bringing it towards us,' said Sindbad.

And then, just as Sherazhad had done earlier, he climbed up and stood on the side of the ship.

'What are you doing?' Connor asked him.

'I'm going to fetch it,' said Sindbad. 'Before it gets too wet. Or sinks.'

'It doesn't matter,' said Connor.

'Yes, it does,' said Sindbad. 'That map's important.'

Sindbad steadied his feet on the narrow wooden planking of the ship's side, bent his knees, and stretched his arms out, making ready to dive. But just before he did, Connor and Sherazhad cried out at the same time.

'Wait!'

'Stop!'

'Look!'

Something was happening to the water around the paper. It was beginning to churn and heave and huge bubbles were rising and bursting on the surface. And as the sea foamed and frothed and seethed it lifted in a great hump of swelling water and the shockwave from it struck the ship so that Connor and Sherazhad stumbled back, and Sindbad was flung down onto the deck. He scrambled to his feet, but the three of them were thrown against each other as the ship rocked violently from side to side. Then, as they were trying to right themselves, there came a sound like thunder booming under the ocean, and a long, loud hissing, then a great roar and crash and the whole ocean seemed to lift upwards in a boiling wall of water that hung suspended for a moment and then came tumbling down upon the ship.

They were hurled across the deck, rolling, scrabbling, sliding, as the ship rocked and reeled again beneath them under the force of the blow. All was heaving and howling water, and cries, and screeching timbers. Then the water began to run away off the decks, and the motion of the ship began to ease, and they were able to pull themselves onto their feet and drag themselves, soaked and gasping, back across to the side.

An awesome sight met their eyes.

Lying in the water a little distance from the ship was a monstrous whale.

It was about twice the length of the ship, high and humped and massive, its skin a dull, greyish white and crisscrossed all over with deep cuts and scars. The scars of many battles, perhaps, fought and won far off and deep down beneath the ocean. Shivers rippled the length of its body beneath its skin, and the sea still churned and foamed about its sides. And just above the surface of the sea, low down in the ancient and battle-scarred creature's huge, square head, a small dark eye gazed at them. And it seemed to Connor there was wicked intelligence in that eye.

Like Connor, Sindbad and Sherazhad were

staring in astonishment at the creature. At last, Sindbad spoke.

'A whale,' he said.

'A white whale,' said Sherazhad.

'And it's big,' said Sindbad.

'It's very big,' said Sherazhad.

'A monster,' said Sindbad.

'It could crush the ship,' said Sherazhad.

Sindbad and Sherazhad looked at each other. Then Sindbad cried out.

'Raise the sails! We have to get away!'

Immediately Sindbad raced across the deck towards the mast. Sherazhad turned to follow him, but before she did, she turned back again quickly to Connor and snapped at him with that fierce, enraged look on her face again.

'You drew a whale on your map!'

Then she ran to help Sindbad unlash the ropes and hoist the sails again.

Connor wanted to shout something after her. It wasn't fair that she kept blaming him for everything that happened. But before he could think of what he would shout, there came another loud, blasting hiss from behind, and he turned to see a jet of air and water rising up from the whale's blowhole and fantailing out in the air, and falling in a feathered mist that sparkled with all the colours of the rainbow. Then the whale began to plough at the waves with its flippers, and it lifted its great tail up out of the water and brought its broad flukes down with a heavy crash that once more sent a great surge of wave crashing into the ship. Connor fell back, and he heard Sindbad and Sherazhad cry out. Water washed over the side and covered him. He rose, spluttering, wiping the stinging salt from his eyes and looked to the middle of the ship. Sindbad was helping Sherazhad to climb out from under the half unfurled sail that had fallen on top of her.

Serves her right, he thought.

Then he went to the side and looked out.

'It's all right,' he called. 'It's going.'

The whale was swimming away from the ship, moving its bulk slowly and steadily through the water.

Sindbad called back to him.

'What did you say?'

'The whale. It's swimming away from the ship.'

Sindbad came and stood next to him. Sherazhad was close behind. They stood at the side, watching the whale moving away.

'There,' said Connor. 'You see?'

Suddenly there was a commotion from the gulls flying around the ship. Connor looked up. They were leaving the ship, and flying in the same direction as the whale. Soon they were above it, and once there, they circled and wheeled in the air, keeping pace with the whale as it swam through the water.

Sindbad inhaled deeply.

'Do you smell it?' he said. 'Land.'

It came strongly and powerfully on the wind, that rich, deep, loamy, earthy smell, almost overpowering. And now Connor, and the others too, realized where it was coming from. The wind was carrying that smell from the direction of the whale.

'That must be an ancient beast,' said Sindbad. 'And it must have travelled to distant lands.' He looked at Connor and Sherazhad. 'Perhaps we should turn the ship about and follow it. It may lead us somewhere.'

Sherazhad was still looking out to sea, and her eyes began to widen.

'There'll be no need for that,' she said. 'It's coming back.'

Connor and Sindbad looked, and gaped in astonishment, and sudden terror. The great white whale was no longer swimming away from them. It had turned, and was now plunging through the water with gathering speed, throwing up a wake on either side of its head, and making straight for the ship.

There was nothing they could do but stand and stare open-mouthed as the beast rushed upon them. Connor's heart was beating furiously, his neck and the back of his hands and all along his spine were a crawling, tingling conglomeration of horrors. He wanted to cry out but his throat was constricted and the cry stuck there like a hard lump of stone. His fingers were closed in a fist and his fingernails digging into his palms. His feet felt as if they'd been hammered through to the deck with nails.

A hand grabbed his arm and pulled at him. It was Sherazhad. She was staring into his face and shouting.

'Get away from the side!'

Then Sindbad grabbed his other arm and all at once the three of them were running back across the deck, stumbling over coils of rope, skidding on the wet planking, trying to get themselves as far away as possible from the terrible impact, when it came, of the whale's head against the ship. And they had only just reached the other side of the ship, and were crouching there, heads tucked down low onto their chests beneath their folded arms, when the impact came.

The huge square head of the whale struck the ship with a shivering blow that knocked Connor off his feet and hurled him across the deck. He knew he must have cried out because he could feel how that cry tore out of his throat, but he couldn't hear it for the sound of the cracking and splitting of the ship's timbers and the roar of the sea as it rushed in. He lay on his front with his arms stretched above him and his fingers scrabbling at the deck as he felt it tilt upwards beneath him and he began to slide backwards. All around him was a rending, wrenching sound, a grinding and a splintering of wood, as if the ghosts of the trees from which the ship had been built had awoken, and were screaming aloud their rage and pain and despair. A great wave washed over him and he gulped seawater that burned his lungs and he lifted his head, to try and breathe, but more seawater poured over him, and he gulped it again. His mind was screaming, 'I'm going to die, I'm going to die, it's not fair, I'm going to die!' as a third wave engulfed him and he felt his fingers loosen their frail grip on the planking, and a dark shape began to flap far back in his head, like a large bat, coming closer, growing bigger, and when the bat-shaped darkness had come right up close and filled him up then he knew he would be dead. And then his mind stopped screaming, and suddenly he was quite calm about it all. If he was going to die, well then, what could he do about it? He wondered vaguely what had become of Sindbad and Shera-zhad. Perhaps they were dead already. Then he wondered if his mother and father would know that he was dead. And then he stopped wondering anything at all. He just seemed to be floating.

But suddenly there came a loud crack and an explosion like a big gun going off and the water that was engulfing him rolled gushing away, and he felt himself being lifted high into the air, his legs dangling down, kicking at emptiness. His hands were holding on to a piece of broken timber and he locked his fingers tight about it, holding on. Then he looked down and found that he was staring at the grey-white, crisscross-marked skin of the whale close to his face. It came to him then what had happened, what was happening. The monster had lifted the broken ship up onto its back and now was plunging forward with it through the water.

Connor clung desperately to his piece of shattered planking, as broken timbers and strips of torn sail and lengths of rope went sliding and tumbling past him. There was a cry in his ear and he caught a brief glimpse of Sindbad's face staring into his, and then it was gone. He heard another cry, which must have been Sherazhad, but it came a long way off, and he didn't see her. Then he was tumbling forwards, as if on a huge slide, or a runaway, out-of-control fairground ride. The planking was torn from his grasp, and everything dropped away, as the whale plunged down into the waves, and here came the ocean again rushing and roaring about him, and beating its deep drum in his ears, and here came the bat-shaped flapping shadow again as he was dragged down, and down, and down, into an endless, spinning, bubbling tunnel of darkness. And all the way down that tunnel his mind was screaming.

Alice put her hands over her ears to try and shut out the sound but it wouldn't go away. She pressed her palms hard into the sides of her head and closed her eyes tight and she was staring into the darkness from which the sound came. Then it was as if there was a mouth in the darkness and the mouth was opening wider and wider and she was falling into the mouth and tumbling down a long throat.

She gave a cry and opened her eyes.

The sound stopped.

She was looking at the room. And everything about the room was the same. Nothing had changed.

But she knew that darkness with its open mouth and long wide throat was still in her head. And that was where her story was going, gulped in by that mouth and swallowed down that throat. And if she wanted to carry on with it that was where she was going to have to go as well.

It's all right, said the Voice.

'Is it?' said Alice.

Yes, said the Voice.

Alice closed her eyes and stared into the darkness. It seemed to be far away from everything, right down at the bottom of the world. She opened her eyes again.

'But where is it?' she said.

You know where, said the Voice.

'It can be,' she said.

It is, said the Voice.

'That's very strange,' she said.

It was strange, but exciting too. She closed her eyes again. And then she opened them quickly.

There was something there, waiting for them, for her, deep in the darkness. And it made her scared.

'What is it?' she said. 'What are they going to find there?'

She waited for an answer.

'What is it?' she said again.

Then the Voice told her.

FOUR
The Pilgrim

There was Sherazhad's voice.

'Perhaps we're in some kind of cave.'

She was speaking from somewhere close by. Over to his left. But he couldn't see her. He couldn't see anything.

'We must be. Yes. Some kind of cave.'

And her voice had a kind of echo to it, a soft whispering that drifted away in vast spaces. So perhaps she was right, they were in some kind of cave. And that was why he couldn't see anything. Because in the cave it was completely dark.

'What kind of cave?'

That was Sindbad's voice, close by as well, and over to his right. And making that same whispered echo.

'Abbu?'

'Sherazhad? Where are you?'

'I'm here. Where are you?'

'Here.'

Their two voices, speaking, whispering across him. He should speak too, he thought, let them know he was here. But he didn't want to. Or he couldn't. He was still feeling dazed, a little strange, as if he'd been somehow knocked out of his body and was only slowly coming back to it, bit by bit. There were his limbs, and his hands and their fingers, and his feet and their toes. All in order, by the feel of them, all in the right place. And there was his back, pressed against the floor of the cave, if a cave was where they were. But there was something odd about the floor. It was firm enough, solid enough, but there was a springiness about it. And a wetness. Not cold but warm, with an oily feel. And it tingled a little.

There came a slithering, squelching sound, first to his right, then to his left.

'Abbu? Are you there?'

Sherazhad's voice, moving in the dark, her feet moving over the wet, springy floor.

'Yes, just here.'

Sindbad moving too, the two of them trying to find each other.

'Where?'

'Here.'

More squelching sounds, and then a gasp, two gasps. Behind him now, above his head. They were standing. He was still lying down. Did they know he was there?

'Where's the boy?'

No, they didn't. That was Sindbad, asking about him. And then Sherazhad answering.

'I don't know.'

And she didn't sound as if she much cared either. He'd better tell them he was here. But that would mean speaking. Would he be able to? Had his voice come back yet along with the rest of it. He decided to try it.

'I'm here.'

'What was that?'

Sindbad sounded startled. Connor spoke again.

'I'm here.'

'Did you hear it?'

'Yes.'

'What was it?'

'It sounded like some kind of squeak.'

No, it wasn't a squeak, it was him, Connor, speaking. Or trying to. His voice hadn't come all the way back yet. He'd have to try harder, make it come back. He spoke again, pushing his voice up out of his throat, stretching his mouth, his lips, to shape the words. Making the voice as loud as he could.

'I'm. Here.'

Two gasps again, startled.

'It's him. The boy.'

'Yes. It's me. Connor.'

'You're here.'

'Yes!'

'Where?'

There was a squelching sound.

'Here—ow!'

He cried out. Someone had stood on his hand.

'Is that you?'

It was Sherazhad.

'Yes.'

'You're lying down. Stand up.'

'I will if you take your foot off my hand.'

She moved. He sat up, then pushed himself to his feet.

'Listen.' Sindbad spoke, standing close by. 'Do you hear that?'

Connor listened, straining his ears into the darkness. And there was a sound coming out of the darkness, a soft, sighing whispered hiss, long and slow, rising and falling and rising again. Hsss. Sshh. Hssss. Sshh. Hsssss. And now that he heard it, he realized that he'd been hearing it ever since he'd come to, but it had been so soft that his mind hadn't registered it as being separate from the darkness itself. But now he realized that it was.

'I hear it,' he said.

'What do you think it is?'

'It's the sea,' said Sherazhad. 'It must be. We're in a cave under the sea, and that's the sound of the sea outside the cave.'

'How did we get here?' said Connor.

'We swam down here,' said Sherazhad. 'After the whale wrecked our ship.'

'I don't remember doing that,' said Connor.

'We must have done,' said Sherazhad.

Connor tried to think, to see if he could remember swimming beneath the sea. But he couldn't. There was the whale smashing into the ship, and that was all. Was it possible? Could they really have swum beneath the sea and found their way to a cave down there?

'We would have drowned,' he said, and it was to himself he said it really, but Sherazhad heard him.

'Yes, but we didn't,' she said, and her voice was very sharp and hard in the dark. 'And we're in a cave, so that's what must have happened.'

The annoying thing was, he couldn't think of any other explanation.

Sindbad had been silent all this time, but now he spoke again.

'There's something else,' he said. 'Another sound.'

Connor listened. Sherazhad stood listening too. They both heard it. From far off, a deep, thumping sound, like a drum being beaten, slow and heavy.

'What's that?' said Connor. 'It's not the sea.'

There was a pause. Then Sherazhad said, 'I don't know.'

They stood, close to each other, but each one alone, in the dark, listening to those sounds, the rise and fall of the soft hiss, the regular, slow thump of the distant drum. Connor's hands were tingling, itching. They were still covered in that oily wetness. He wiped them dry on his jeans. Was it really a cave they were in? Sindbad seemed to be having the same thought.

'It would help if we could see something,' he said. 'If there was just a little light.'

And then there was.

It came slowly, the solid darkness beginning to crumble, to curl and drift like twists of smoke, breaking up into specks of floating ash, letting the light through. A dull light, that didn't come from any particular direction, but from all around. And by that dull light they saw that they were standing in what appeared to be some huge cavern, with a long, curved, ridged ceiling high above them, and curved and ridged walls of smooth, glistening rock.

'You were right,' Connor said to Sherazhad. 'We're in a cave.'

'A cavern beneath the sea,' said Sherazhad.

Connor gazed at the walls and ceiling of the cavern. They were glowing with the light, which had grown a little brighter now, but he noticed something else about them as well. They seemed to be moving, pulsing gently, almost as if they were alive. They couldn't be, of course, he realized that. So perhaps it was the light itself that was pulsating. But where was the light coming from? From the walls themselves? How could the walls glow like that? The more he stared at them, the stranger they appeared to him, and the more uneasy he became.

And then he remembered that he had read

somewhere, or seen on a television programme, something about certain kinds of undersea creatures and plants that had their own phosphorescent light. That must be what he could see pulsating, creatures or plants like that, living on the walls of the cavern, their skins glowing in the dark.

That made him feel a little easier. But it still didn't explain how they'd come to be in the cavern.

Perhaps, he thought, the same way as I fell into the map.

'What's that?'

Connor turned at the sound of Sindbad's voice. He was leaning forward a little, peering into the gloomy light. Connor and Sherazhad followed his gaze. At the far end of the cavern, where one of the walls sloped down to the floor, there was an over-hang a little way above the floor. All was shadowy beneath the overhang, but shining out from some-where among those shadows was a small, flickering light. Not like the light that glowed from the walls. It was more like the light of a candle flame.

They looked at each other.

'There can't be anyone else down here,' said Connor.

'Why not?' said Sherazhad. 'We are.'

'Let's go and see,' said Sindbad.

'And be ready for whatever we find,' said Sherazhad, and drew her knife from her sash. And this time Connor was glad she did.

They set off walking across the smooth, wet floor, treading carefully because it was so oily and slippery. The water, or whatever liquid it was that covered the floor, made a soft, sucking sound as they walked.

'My feet are tingling,' said Sherazhad.

'So are mine,' said Sindbad.

They were both barefooted. Connor was wearing his trainers and felt nothing through them. But there was still a vague tingling sensation in his hands.

As they drew nearer to the wall they began to make out something tucked away beneath the overhang, some kind of bulky shape, and that the flickering light came from somewhere from within this shape. And as they drew nearer still they realized that indeed they weren't the only ones in that undersea cavern, for someone had built a hut there. It was a leaning, tumbledown, ramshackle construction of pieces of ship's planking lashed together with lengths of frayed rope and ripped sailcloth. The whole thing seemed to have been squashed tight up against the roof of the overhang and the back wall, probably to prevent it from collapsing. A piece of tattered, threadbare sacking hung across the front. The light from the candle flame showed through the sacking.

They stopped a little way from the overhang. When they spoke they kept their voices low.

'There's only one at least,' said Sherazhad. 'That hut's not big enough for more.'

'Sometimes one can be enough,' said Sindbad.

'Not for us,' said Sherazhad. 'Not for me and my knife.' She pressed its point with the ball of her thumb.

'You're right,' said Sindbad. 'Three of us, and one of him.'

'Or her,' said Sherazhad.

'Or it,' said Connor.

Sindbad and Sherazhad stared at him.

'We don't know what's in there,' he said. 'Whoever built that hut might have died a long time ago. He might be just bones by now. And something came along to eat the bones. And that something's in there now, waiting for us . . . '

He stopped. He stared at Sindbad and Sherazhad, staring at him. By the looks on their faces he seemed to have frightened them. He'd certainly frightened himself. He had no idea where that idea had come from. It seemed to have just sprung into his mind from nowhere. As if it hadn't come from him at all. It was more like something his sister would say, when she was telling one of her strange stories.

'The light's still burning.'

'What?'

Sherazhad's voice had brought him back. She nodded towards the hut.

'That candle, inside the hut, it's still burning. That means somebody human is keeping it alight. And not some creature that eats people's bones.'

'Yes,' said Sindbad. 'You're right.' Then he lifted the curved, broad-bladed sword that hung from a loop at his side. 'Even so,' he said. 'We'd best not take chances.'

He walked slowly towards the overhang and the hut. Sherazhad and Connor went with him, walking on either side. Sherazhad held the blade of her knife forward. Connor had his fists clenched, in an effort to stop himself from trembling.

At last they stood before the hut. They listened. No sound came from inside. They could see no movement or form through the sacking. Only the flickering glow of the flame. Connor wondered suddenly if this might be a trap, set there deliberately to lure them inside. That all the time something was watching, waiting for them to make their move. And then it would pounce. But it was a fleeting thought and came too late, because Sindbad had already placed the point of his sword beneath the corner of the sacking and was lifting it up.

He stooped, and peered inside the hut. Then he looked back at Connor and Sherazhad.

'I think it's safe,' he said, and pulled the sacking right back and went inside. Sherazhad and Connor went in after him.

The light came not from a candle but from a lantern. It hung from a hook in the ceiling and cast a guttering red light on the interior. In one of the corners stood a few barrels and wooden crates. And on the bare wooden floor a figure lay wrapped in sailcloth.

It lay in shadow and no sound came from it. Sindbad took the lantern from the hook and lowered it towards the figure. Then they saw that it was a man, or had been a man, for it appeared now not to be breathing. Only its face was exposed and the hands folded across its chest, and these were thin and bony and gaunt. The head completely hairless. And the skin stretched tight across the face and the hands was pale and dry-looking, a blotched and mottled white, as if all colour had been drained from it. The guttering flame in the lantern threw circles of dark shadow around the shut and sunken eyes, and its red light gave a flickering animation to the apparently lifeless features.

Connor gazed at those features with a mixture of horror and fascination. It was like a face staring back at him out of a nightmare, the kind of nightmare that the sleeping part of you knows is just a bad dream, but even so you just can't wake up from it. In the same way, Connor knew that he couldn't look away from that face. So he went on looking at it, as Sindbad and Sherazhad spoke across him.

'Whoever this poor man was, he appears to be no more.'

'You mean he's dead.'

'He doesn't look to be living.'

'How long do you think he's been like this?'

'A long time, I'd say.'

'Then what about the lantern, Abbu?'

'The lantern?'

'Who has kept the flame burning?'

There was silence for a few moments. Connor felt, but did not see, Sindbad look at Sherazhad. He was still staring at the face, and it was like that part in the nightmare where things are going to get even worse and still you won't be able to wake up. Then the flamelight on the figure's face grew brighter as Sindbad lowered the lantern.

The shadows around the eyesockets flickered.

The bony fingers seemed to twitch.

And there was a sudden rasp of indrawn breath and the eyes snapped open.

Alice was shaking her head. She had her hands clasped over her eyes.

'No, no, no,' she was saying. 'I don't like it. Take it away. I don't want it in my story.'

The Voice was trying to speak to her but she wasn't listening to it. She just kept on shaking her head and hiding her eyes and saying, over and over again, 'No, no, no, no, no.'

It was the face. She didn't like the face. The Voice had made the face appear and now she wanted the Voice to make it go away again.

'No, no, no.'

But the Voice wasn't going to make the face go away. That's what it was trying to tell her. That the face was part of the story, just like everything else. The face had to be there. The story couldn't go on without the face being there.

But Alice didn't want to hear what the Voice was telling her. She didn't want the face to be there. It made her afraid. Just like when she saw it looking out of the window in the tower.

'No, no, no, no.'

And then she stopped. She sat upright and snatched her hands away from her eyes. She stared ahead, startled.

The Voice had spoken sharply to her. And it had been like having a small electric shock. A tiny crackle of lightning snapping inside her head. It hadn't hurt, but it had taken her completely by surprise. So now she sat, silent, as the Voice carried on speaking. It told her how she must listen to it. That was very important. If she didn't listen, things might start to go wrong with the story. And things must not go wrong with the story. That too was very important.

And the face, that face that made her afraid, that had to be in the story.

Did she understand? Did she agree?

Alice nodded. She understood. She agreed.

Good, said the Voice. Now we can go on.

* * *

109

The man stared at them. His eyes seemed filled with a wild light, darting from Connor, to Sherazhad, to Sindbad, and back to Connor again. Then he spoke, his voice a harsh, grating whisper, like dry sand and pebbles running through a sieve. And there was a darting wildness in his words as well.

'Are we there yet?' he said.

And then, 'What are you doing here?'

And then, 'Who am I?'

And then suddenly he sat up and pushed his face towards Connor, and Connor felt bony fingers grasp hold of the front of his T-shirt and found himself fixed by the man's wild, staring eyes.

'And you? Who are you?'

Connor tried to pull free but the fingers were locked tight. And the hard, glittering light that shone from the eyes seemed to be boring into him, like two sharp needles, pressing in deeper, and deeper.

Then the man gave a gasp and let go of Connor's T-shirt. Connor stood back. Sherazhad was holding the point of her knife against the man's throat.

'I'll tell you who we are,' she said. 'This man is none other than Al-Sindbaad Al-Bahri, known also as Sindbad, King of the Pirates. And I am Sherazhad, his fearsome daughter. We are the torments and terrors of the Eastern Seas. Where we pass, the waves are red with blood, and all quake in terror at the mention of our names.'

The man sat looking at her as if waiting for her to

go on. Connor saw no fear in that pale, gaunt face, and he seemed unconcerned by the knife against his throat. Sherazhad too sensed this, and for a moment she seemed to falter, and the knife blade trembled in her grip. But then she recovered herself, and spoke again, even more fiercely.

'Speak, and speak only the truth,' she said. 'If you lie we'll know it. And if you lie, a moment later I'll cut your throat.'

Still the man gazed at her calmly, and his voice when he spoke, though still with its dry whisper, was calm as well. The wild and startled panic of only a few moments ago seemed entirely to have left him.

'What is it you want to know?'

'Who you are.'

'He doesn't know who he is,' said Sindbad. 'He said that.'

Sherazhad frowned. The man spoke again.

'And I can't tell you anything with your knife at my throat.'

He continued to gaze at her steadily. The light from the lantern that Sindbad was holding flashed across them, and Connor saw that they were a pale, icy blue, and there was no fear in them.

'Yes,' said Sindbad. 'Put your knife away. I don't think there's any danger here.'

He fitted his own sword back into its loop, but Sherazhad waited a moment or two more before she took her knife away and slid it beneath her

111

sash. They both took a step back and the man gave a thin smile. Then he turned once more to Connor.

'Would you get me some water?' he said. 'There's a barrel there in the corner.'

Connor went to where the barrels and crates stood in the corner. The barrels were similar to those on board Sindbad's ship, and one of them was about a quarter full of stale-smelling water. He carried it across to the centre of the hut and set it down. The man knelt up and reached into the barrel with one hand and cupped some water to his mouth. He sucked it noisily from his palm, then did the same again, and then a third time. At last, when he was finished, he looked up.

'Sit down,' he said, and though he'd quenched his thirst, his voice still had that rasping, whispered quality. 'I'll tell you all you want to know. And you can tell me.'

They sat. The man unwound the sailcloth from his shoulders and let it fall. He wore a simple, plain gown of some rough-looking material, stained and ragged and frayed. His feet were bare. Like his hands, they were thin, bony, the skin mottled and pale. From the glimpses Connor had through the tattered gown, the rest of his body was the same. It was impossible to tell what age he was.

For some moments the man sat with his face lowered, gazing at the floor, then he looked up sharply, and his eyes with their cold, sharp light passed across each of them in turn. Then he spoke.

'I was confused when you first woke me,' he said. 'It's no surprise. I don't know how long I was sleeping for. Nor how long I've been here. Days. Weeks. I can't tell.' He glanced at the lantern, which Sindbad had placed between them on the floor, so that its light caught all their faces. 'That's still burning, so it can't have been that long. But who can tell? Time may have stopped, and started again. In this world anything can happen.'

When he said that, Sindbad and Sherazhad glanced at each other, and Connor remembered how time had seemed to stop for them on board the ship, and then start again. They said nothing, but the man had seen that glance.

'You know something of that?' he said. 'You know you are in a world that is not your own?'

He looked directly at Connor when he said this, and once more he felt the light in the man's eyes pierce him through. It made him uncomfortable, as if the man was somehow looking deep inside him, searching for something there. He wanted to look away but he couldn't. The man's stare held him as firmly as he had held him with his bony fingers a little while before. And once again Sherazhad came to his rescue.

'We're asking the questions.'

Her voice was as sharp as her knifeblade, and the

man turned his eyes from Connor. Connor relaxed, as if from a grip round his throat, or his heart.

'Of course you are,' whispered the man. 'And you have many questions to ask, I shouldn't wonder. Probably more than can be answered.'

'We'll start with a simple one,' she said. 'What's your name?'

Just before he spoke, something flickered across his face. A shadow, a wisp of smoke. Perhaps from the lantern-flame, perhaps from some other, more secret source.

'My name,' he said, and paused, then spoke it. 'Is Trismagistus.'

'Trismagistus,' said Sindbad.

The man looked at him.

'You know the name?' he said.

Sindbad shook his head.

'No. I've never heard a name like it before.'

'Oh.' Trismagistus seemed a little disappointed. 'Well,' he said. 'You've heard it now. Trismagistus.' He spoke it himself, in his dry voice, as if he were tasting it, wetting his lips with his tongue, as if the name itself was nourishment for him. 'Trismagistus,' he said again. 'And I am, or was, and perhaps still am, a pilgrim. A traveller. Journeying across the world, across all the worlds, in search of wonders.'

'Worlds?' said Sindbad. 'More than one?'

'Of course more than one,' said Trismagistus. 'You know that. This world, the one we are in, is not

your own.' He was looking at Sherazhad and Sindbad, but now once more, with a movement as quick
as a snake, he turned to Connor. 'And it is not yours.
You have come here from some other. As they have.
Theirs is a world of sea-voyages, of pirates. If that is
what they are.'

'It is!' said Sherazhad fiercely. 'Isn't it, Abbu?'

'Oh, yes,' said Sindbad. 'Pirates. Yes. Certainly.'
He grinned broadly as he said it, and didn't look at
all fierce. Trismagistus looked at him, smiled his thin
smile, then turned back to Connor.

'But their world,' he said, 'is not your world. Is it?'

Connor knew he had to speak, that Trismagistus wanted to know his story, and for some reason
wanted to know that most of all.

'No,' he said. 'It's not.'

'And what was it brought you here?' said Trismagistus.

'You're doing it again,' said Sherazhad. 'Asking
the questions. You'll find out about us after we've
found out about you.'

Once more, with that snakelike swiftness, Trismagistus turned on Sherazhad and his voice hissed
as if he was himself a snake about to strike.

'And what do you think gives you the right—?' he
began, but was silenced by the flash of light from the
blade of her knife which once more she was holding
towards his throat. She was glaring at him but he
held her gaze. 'Take the knife away,' he said.

Sherazhad said nothing, and this time her grip on the knife did not falter. It was Sindbad who spoke.

'Do as he says, Sherazhad. It serves no purpose.'

She held the knife there a moment longer, then lowered it and pushed it back once more into her sash. But still kept her eyes on Trismagistus.

'Now,' said Sindbad. 'If you'll be so good, perhaps you would tell us how you came to be in this cave.'

Trismagistus looked at Sindbad. His eyes widened, flashed, and he gave a sharp, rasping laugh.

'A cave!' he said. 'You think we're in a cave!'

'Aren't we?' said Sindbad.

Trismagistus sat forward. He folded his hands together. He smiled his thin smile. His pale, hairless head gleamed in the lantern light. His voice was a soft, dry whisper.

'How did you come to be here?'

'We asked you,' said Sherazhad.

'And now I'm asking you,' said Trismagistus. Still the soft whisper, but with an edge to it and an authority more potent than any knife blade. 'It's important you answer.'

'There was a whale,' said Sindbad.

'A whale!' he said. 'What kind of whale! What did it look like? Let me see if I can guess. Whiteish coloured, maybe. Its body cut and criss-crossed all over with old scars. A whale of monstrous size, and monstrous wickedness.'

Connor saw again the creature rising from the ocean, saw it rushing towards them through the waves, intent on destroying them.

'You've seen it too,' he said.

Trismagistus turned to him.

'Yes,' he said. 'I've seen it.'

And he gave a low, grating laugh. Then he said, 'And what happened when you saw this whale?'

'It rammed our ship,' said Sindbad. 'Smashed it to pieces.'

'And we were thrown into the sea,' said Sherazhad.

Trismagistus's eyes glittered hard and cold and bright.

'And then what?' he said. 'What happened to you then? Let me guess again. You were dragged down beneath the ocean. Down and down and down, into the dark. Swallowed whole.'

A horrible fear began to grip at Connor's heart and squeeze it tight.

'Swallowed?' said Sindbad. 'What do you mean?'

Once again that burst of harsh laughter came from his throat, almost a cry of triumph, and the wild light flashed in his shadow-pooled eyes. Then he leaned forward and spoke, and the scratch of his voice was like fingernails dragged over dry stone. 'Lister. Do you hear it? Do you hear where you are?'

They listened. Connor listened. And he heard, and they heard, those sounds that had been with

117

them since they'd woken. The soft, whispered hush, rising and falling. The far off, slow, heavy drumbeat. Living sounds. And suddenly he knew, as suddenly they knew, with an awful, sickening realization, what place it was they had woken to. Even as Trismagistus spoke.

'You hear the blood in its veins. You hear the beating of its heart. You know where you are. This is no cave. This is the belly of the whale.'

They stared at Trismagistus. He gazed back at them. The lamplight guttered across his face, stripes of red flame and shadow, across the pale and hairless dome of his head. More like a mask than a real face, Connor thought. And the thought made him shudder inside.

'Inside the whale,' said Sherazhad. 'It's not possible.'

'You think I'm lying?' said Trismagistus.

'I think you're mad,' said Sherazhad.

Trismagistus looked at Sindbad.

'Do you think I'm mad?'

'I don't know,' said Sindbad.

'Go and look,' said Trismagistus. 'See for yourselves. Look again at the walls of this cave.'

Sherazhad stood and went to the entrance. She drew back the cloth that hung there and looked out. Then she stepped out of the hut. Sindbad followed her. Trismagistus turned to Connor.

'You're not going with them?'

Connor shook his head. Trismagistus smiled and leaned in closer to him. He looked deep into Connor's eyes, and once again Connor felt the needle-sharp light of those eyes boring into him, deep into his brain.

'You know, don't you?' said Trismagistus. 'You know it's true. It's all real.'

Connor was pinned down by those eyes and couldn't look away.

'Yes,' he said. 'I know.'

And Trismagistus leaned in even closer, so that all that Connor could see now were those eyes, and the hard light in those eyes, probing even deeper, into the back of his skull. And when Trismagistus spoke again his voice had the sound of feet treading softly on dry leaves and twigs.

'And you know even more than that.'

There was movement. The cloth in front of the entrance was pulled back. Sindbad and Sherazhad entered. Trismagistus turned to them. The needles drew back from Connor's brain.

'Are your feet tingling?' said Trismagistus.

It was an unexpected question. Connor remembered the tingling feeling in his hands.

'Yes,' said Sindbad. 'They are.'

'The juices,' said Trismagistus.

'Juices?' said Sherazhad.

'Digestive juices,' said Trismagistus.

Sindbad and Sherazhad looked at each other, then at their feet, then at Trismagistus again.

'It begins with a tingling,' said Trismagistus. 'You don't notice it at first. Then it begins to burn, and the burning gets worse, and then it begins to burn the colour off your skin. That's what happened to me. The tingling, the burning. Then I realized what was happening. I was being slowly digested.'

He was sitting forward, his hands with their long, bony white fingers pressed into his knees, his voice no more than the scratch of whisper. Connor felt a slow horror creeping under his skin.

'Luckily there was the boat. Wrecked, of course, but from the wreckage I built this shelter. And here I stayed. And here I stay.'

He lifted his hands, locked his fingers together, cracked them, and laid his hands once more upon his knees. Connor noticed that his fingers had no nails.

'Where did the boat come from?' said Sindbad.

'From the ship.'

'And the ship?'

'Wrecked by the whale.'

'As ours was,' said Sherazhad.

Sindbad and Sherazhad were still standing at the entrance to the hut. Now Sherazhad came forward so that she stood above Trismagistus.

'Tell us what happened to you,' she said. 'Tell us your story.'

Connor noticed that the fierceness was gone from her voice. She seemed as shaken and unnerved as he was by the whole experience. And by Trismagistus too.

'Of course,' said Trismagistus. 'Sit.'

Sherazhad sat. Sindbad came across and sat beside her. He crossed his legs and scratched at the soles of his feet. Then scratched them again. Trismagistus scooped up some of the water from the barrel and sucked it from his cupped palm. Drops spilled between his fingers, from the corners of his mouth, his chin. Then he looked up at them and spoke.

'As I've already told you I was, I am, a pilgrim, seeking out the wonders of the worlds. And I was making what I hoped would be my final voyage, which would take me to the greatest wonder of them all. A long voyage, it would be, to the very ends of the earth. I fitted the ship myself, hired the crew, we set sail on a day of fair weather. Soon we were out of sight of land, and only the open ocean before us. But as we sailed on, the crew became uneasy. They had never journeyed so far from land before, and feared they would never return. I saw their sidelong glances, heard their low murmurings as I passed them on the deck. More than once a muttered curse. I knew trouble was coming. And at last it did. I woke one morning to the sound of my cabin door being broken open, and several members of the crew bursting in, all armed. They dragged me from my cabin, took me up on deck. The whole crew were assembled there. They told me they had sailed far enough, would sail no further. They were taking the ship over, turning it round, and heading back for home. And they weren't taking me with them. They put me in a boat with a sail, and water, and a little dried food, and lowered me over the side. So I was cast adrift in the middle of that great uncharted ocean. I sailed on alone. I don't know how long for. But I had drunk the last of the water when I saw land ahead of me. I thought at first this was the country I was searching for, but as I drew closer I saw it was an island. My heart lifted, though, because there were trees and bushes growing on the island, and as I drew closer I could hear the song of birds among the leaves. Songs I had never heard any bird sing before. Songs I shall never forget, though I never saw the birds that sang them.'

Trismagistus paused and dipped his hand once more into the barrel to drink. Connor looked at Shera-zhad. She was sitting forward, her eyes wide, shining with the glow from the lamp. He could see that she was entranced by Trismagistus's story. By Trismagistus himself. So was Sindbad. And so was he. All of them spellcast by the tale, and the voice that told it.

Trismagistus continued.

'I drew near the island, got out, and pulled the boat ashore. Not only were there trees on the island, but fruit growing on the branches of those trees, and a pool of clear water among them. I gathered fruit, filled up the water barrel, sat beneath the shade of trees, ate, and drank, and listened to the magical singing of those hidden birds. It was like a paradise. The sun began to go down. I decided to stay there the night before going on. I broke branches from the trees and lit a fire. I sat close to the flames as it grew dark. But then I felt a tremor run through the island, and there came a rumbling sound, and the island shook, and shook again. I was flung onto my back as the ground beneath me heaved upwards. Trees were uprooted and came crashing down. I heard the voices of the birds shrieking in terror and panic as they took flight. The island rose up beneath me, lifting higher and higher out of the water. My boat slid off and crashed into the sea. The earth in which those trees had been growing fell away. And then I realized that the island had been no island, and that I was clinging to the back of a gigantic whale. The monstrous white whale. How long must it have lain there sleeping in the ocean, for earth to settle on its back, for the seeds of trees and bushes to take root and grow? Perhaps from the days when the world was young. But now the fire I had lit had awoken it, and it was in a rage. It thrashed its body through the ocean, churning up mountainous waves, throwing me this way and that, until finally I was flung into those boiling waves. I sank and rose to the surface again, and saw that I was close to my boat. It was capsized, but I swam to it, and pulled myself up onto its upturned keel. I thought if I could stay there until the whale had swum away, or dived beneath the ocean, then I would be saved. But all at once I felt the sea rock and shudder once more, and turned to see the whale rushing upon me, its jaws gaping wide. There was nothing I could do. I closed my eyes and waited. And then there was a roaring. And there was darkness. And then I woke and I was here.'

He was silent. His story was finished. For a while no one spoke. Connor felt unable to. The spell of that voice was still upon him. It seemed that way for the others too. But at last Sherazhad did speak.

'That's a fantastic story.'

'Not too fantastic, I hope,' said Trismagistus.

'Is it true?'

'Is yours?'

'Yes,' she said.

Trismagistus smiled.

'Then so is mine.'

Sindbad was watching Trismagistus. Connor noticed that he was frowning a little, a quizzical look in his eyes. He looked as if he was about to speak, then seemed to change his mind, and sat back. But then he leaned forward again.

'This voyage of yours. You said it was to seek out the greatest wonder of the world.'

'Of all the worlds,' said Trismagistus.

'What is it? This great wonder?'

Trismagistus paused for a moment. Then he said: 'It's called the Tower of Truth.'

The words slammed into Connor's brain like a fist. His body reeled with the blow. Sindbad and Sherazhad both gasped. Trismagistus sat up, alert.

'You know it?' he said. 'You've heard of it?'

Sherazhad looked across at Connor.

'He knows about it,' she said.

Trismagistus turned to him, and there was an urgency in his eyes, his voice.

'What do you know of it?'

Connor found it hard to speak. His throat was dry.

'It was on a map,' he said.

Trismagistus's hand leapt out and grabbed his wrist.

'A map. What kind of map? Where did you find it? Tell me. Tell me about the map.'

The bony fingers were biting into Connor's flesh.

'You're hurting me,' he said.

Trismagistus looked down at his own hand, as if he hadn't even realized what it was doing. He loosed Connor's wrist.

'I'm sorry,' he said. 'But you don't know—it's important that you tell me about the map—about the Tower—not just for me—for you—all of us.' He was trying to make his voice as gentle as he could. 'It may help us escape from this dreadful place.'

'I knew it was all his fault,' said Sherazhad.

'Leave that now,' said Sindbad. Then to Connor, in a kinder voice. 'Tell him what you told us.'

Connor nodded.

'Can I have a drink of water first?'

'Of course,' said Trismagistus.

He pushed the barrel closer to Connor. Connor cupped his hand in the water and drank. The water was foul-tasting, and he had to swallow hard to make it go down. But at least his throat didn't feel so dry now.

'Right,' he said.

Then he told his story, from discovering the map in the book, to the storm, and finding himself on board the ship. Sindbad helped him then, joining in with the rest of the story, up to the wrecking of the ship by the whale. And throughout it all Trismagistus sat absolutely still, listening with great intensity, eyes wide and unblinking. And when at last the story was finished he continued to sit unmoving, his eyes fixed on Connor, as if waiting for more, as if somehow knowing that not all had been told.

And it hadn't been. As when he'd told the story to Sindbad and Sherazhad, Connor hadn't spoken of his sister, or of her scribbling on the map, or his kicking over of her tower.

Did Trismagistus know that? Could those eyes see that far into his brain?

Connor looked away, down at his hands. But he could still feel Trismagistus looking at him. And then he heard him speak, a single crack in the bone dry voice.

'Strange.'

Connor looked at his hands.

'Yes, it is. Everything.'

'Not just that,' said Trismagistus, and it was so quiet, his voice, a slow wind stirring through fallen leaves. 'Why you?' Like a creature creeping through those leaves upon its prey. 'Why should it bring you here?' Closer and closer, ready to pounce. 'What did you do?' Connor knew he would have to look up. And he did. And saw those eyes looking into him. And was about to speak. When suddenly Sherazhad cried out.

'It burned me!'

They all turned to her. She cried out again.

'It's burning!'

'What is?' said Sindbad.

Sherazhad winced and gasped in pain and grabbed at something down by her side, then gasped again and scrabbled with her fingers at the knot in her sash, and pulled it loose and flung it away from her.

It landed on the wooden floor with a thud. And there lay the sash with the bottle attached. The bottle which she had found in the hold of the ship when she was looking for some paper for Connor.

The one they hadn't been able to open.

'That!' said Sherazhad, and she was staring at the bottle, as they all were. 'And look at it.'

They were all staring at the bottle. It was glowing. The red clay from which it was made burning brighter, deeper, as if from some flame lit within. Yet even as they watched, the glow dimmed, grew faint, and died.

'Where did you find that bottle?' said Trismagistus.

'In the hold of our ship,' said Sherazhad.

'I'd never seen it before,' said Sindbad.

Connor remembered how it had burned his hand when he had stumbled upon it in the dark of the hold. Sherazhad too had spoken of it burning her when she had found it.

'What's in it?'

'I don't know,' said Sherazhad. 'I couldn't open it. And with all that's happened since it slipped my mind.'

'Let's try opening it now,' said Trismagistus.

He reached out a skinny hand to take hold of the bottle. But at the same moment a white spark crackled and jumped inside Connor's head and his body jerked and the next thing he knew he was holding the bottle in his hand. It was cool beneath his skin and gave off no heat.

'I'll do it,' he said.

He looked up at Trismagistus. Trismagistus

smiled at him.

'Go on, then,' he said.

The stopper was pushed in deep. It was made of the same baked clay as the bottle. He clamped his finger and thumb around it and twisted and pulled. It didn't move. He laid the bottle on the floor and held it down with his left hand and pulled again at the stopper with the fingers of his right hand. Still it didn't move. He was aware of the others leaning close over him.

'Give me room,' he said.

They sat back, and he hooked the knuckles of the first two fingers of his hand over the top of the stopper and twisted round to the left, straining the weight of the bottle against his wrist. His thumb pushed into the neck to give more leverage. A sharp pain stabbed through the tendons of his wrist as he felt them tauten and his wristbone lock. The stopper grated against the inside of the neck, and stuck, and grated again and turned a little more, and then he could feel it easing, loosening, and finally it gave, and turned in his fingers and he pulled and it was out.

He dropped the stopper onto the floor.

'What's inside?' said Sindbad.

Connor picked up the bottle and held the opening in the neck close to his eye.

'I can't see.'

There was a gutter of light across his face, across the bottle. Trismagistus was holding up the lamp.

'Look again,' he said.

Connor angled the opening towards the lamp so that it caught its glow, and he could see into it. It seemed empty. He angled the bottle again, and now saw that there was some kind of cylinder inside the bottle, and that the thin edges of this cylinder ran around the inside of the neck. He pushed in with his forefinger and pressed against the cylinder. It gave beneath his probing. He placed his thumb against the outside of the neck and crooked his forefinger against the cylinder and then pulled upwards. The top of the cylinder slid up above the neck and it wasn't a cylinder. It was a roll of some stiff, dark-coloured paper.

He held the bottle away from him, with the roll of paper sticking out of it. There was a humming sound coming from deep inside his brain and he realized that he had been hearing it for some time. He eased the roll out of the bottle. Then he put the bottle down and took the roll of paper in both hands and opened it out. And he knew what it was before he did that.

It was the map.

FIVE

The Desert

Alice was looking at the map. She was standing at the table in front of the window and she was frowning. Her hair hung in tangles around her face. One of the tangles fell across her eyes and she blew at it then brushed it aside. The storm outside had passed now and the mass of dark cloud had broken and was drifting apart. There was a wet shine off the wreckage of the garden. The sunlight through the window cast a bright shaft across the table and the map. She bent a little closer and placed her finger on the place where Connor had drawn the ship.

That had been a terrible storm and very frightening. She was pleased with it and she was pleased with the pirates as well because although they seemed to be frightening they weren't really. She liked the girl and the name she'd found for her from the book, even though she couldn't say it properly. The girl was wild and savage and not scared of anything and she wanted to do brave things. The other one wanted to do brave things as well, and they would, both of them, although she wasn't sure

131

what yet. The Voice would tell her when the time came.

But for the time being the Voice was quiet. Quite suddenly it had stopped speaking. She had sat and waited for it to start again because she wanted to go on with the story, but it hadn't. So then she had stood up and come across to the table to look at the map. She was looking at the map and waiting for the Voice to speak to her, to help her go on with the story. She needed the Voice for that. But somehow she knew that the Voice needed her as well. Perhaps that's why the Voice had gone quiet. Perhaps it was waiting for her to think of the next thing.

She moved her finger up the paper to the whale. The whale's tail. The Voice called them flukes. She hadn't heard that word before and she liked it. She said it out loud.

'Flukes.'

She smiled. It made a good sound. She said it again.

'Flukes. The whale's flukes.'

Yes.

She looked at the flukes sticking up out of the water, and thought of the rest of the whale under the water, and then she thought of the whale lying down there deep beneath the ocean and what it would be like to be in its belly. Horrible. And frightening too. More frightening than the storm. But that was partly because he was there. The man with the horrible face. She still didn't like him, but the Voice was right, he had to be in the story. It wouldn't work without him.

He wasn't doing much to make it work at the moment though. Nobody was. They were stuck. And she had to get them out of there. They couldn't stay in the whale's belly. It was time for them to leave, go somewhere else. But where? Perhaps that's why the Voice was quiet. It was waiting for her to decide where they should go next, and then it would start speaking and tell her how to get them there.

Right then.

She looked at the top of the paper, where Connor had drawn the island with the tower. The tower she had scribbled over. She looked at those angry, thick, black, ugly pencil marks. She wished she could take them away, put it right. She'd spoiled the tower, and spoiling the tower had spoiled the whole map. The tower was the most important thing on the map.

Then her eyes widened with excitement and her heart beat a little faster. A thrill ran through her. That was it! That's what the story was about. Getting rid of those scratchmarks. Making the tower right again. So that was where they should go next.

'Ow!'

She snatched her hand away from the paper. Her finger had been burned. Just a small burn, but sharp enough to make her cry out. And at the same time, the Voice spoke.

Not there. Not yet. Somewhere else first.

Alice put her burned finger in her mouth and sucked it. She stood at the table with her head down, frowning.

Stop sulking, the Voice said. It didn't hurt that much. And it's not hurting at all now.

Its voice was stern, like her mother's or father's when she was being told off. And she didn't like being told off. She kept her finger in her mouth and frowned harder. Her hair was hanging over her eyes and she left it there. The Voice spoke again.

All right. We'll leave it there. We won't carry on with the story. We'll just leave everything as it is.

Alice lifted her head. She waited for the Voice to speak again. It didn't. Slowly she took her finger out of her mouth and dropped her hand to her side.

That's better, said the Voice, and it was kinder now. And then it said, I can't make this story without you.

Alice smiled.

'Right, then,' she said. 'Where shall we take them to?'

Look on the map.

Alice looked.

There was a large country lower down. Alice knew that countries towards the south were hotter than countries in the north. This must be one of those hot countries. It looked completely empty, except for what looked like a heap of broken stones in the middle.

'What's here?' she said.

The Voice answered her straight away.

A desert. And other things.

'What other things?'

Things that live in the desert.

Alice shuddered with delight. She had no idea what those things might be but she wanted to find out, and she knew that she would find out if they took the story there.

'All right,' she said. 'Let's go there.'

She put her finger on the map.

Connor was looking at the map. He had placed it on the floor and was kneeling above it holding it out flat with his hands. Sindbad and Sherazhad were sitting to his right, leaning over. Trismagistus was on his left.

'Is it the same?' he said. 'Is it the same as the one you found?'

Connor squinted through the gloom.

'I can't see,' he said.

It was about the same size as the one he'd found, and of the same thick paper. The outlines of the countries appeared to be the same as well but in the dim half light he couldn't make out any of the details.

'Just a moment.'

Trismagistus reached across and picked up the lantern and held it up over the map. Its flame cast a flickering glow across its surface. Connor and

Trismagistus both gasped at the same time.

'The Tower!' said Trismagistus.

'What is it?' said Sindbad. 'What's the matter?'

Connor was staring at the island at the top of the world. The island where the Tower had stood. On this map the island was empty. He couldn't speak.

Trismagistus pointed a single, thin finger towards the empty space.

'It's gone,' he said. 'It was there. The Tower. This is where it stood.'

Connor saw the finger with its pale, nail-less tip brush lightly at the surface of the map.

'Not there,' said Trismagistus. 'But why? What happened to it?'

Connor knew that Trismagistus was speaking to him. He didn't dare look up. He shook his head.

'I don't know,' he said.

And he could feel the eyes looking at him, trying to drive their glittering points into and through the top of his head. And he knew that those eyes didn't believe him. He was relieved when Sherazhad spoke.

'This isn't the same map, is it?' she said. 'As the one you found?'

Connor looked up at her.

'No,' he said. 'It's different.'

'That's it, then,' she said. 'Perhaps this map was made before the Tower was built.'

'Impossible.' The lantern shook in Trismagistus's hand and the light splashed and rippled across his face as he leaned forward. 'The Tower was there before any map was made. There is no map of this world on which the Tower does not stand.'

'It's not on this map,' said Sindbad.

'And it's only a map,' said Sherazhad. 'It doesn't mean the Tower isn't there in the world.'

'You don't understand,' said Trismagistus. 'What is shown on the map is there in the world. The map shows the world as it truly is.'

Sherazhad stared for some moments at the map. Then she looked up at Trismagistus.

'You're right,' she said. 'I don't understand.'

'The map of the world, and the world itself, are one.'

'And I still don't,' she said, and turned to Sindbad. 'Do you understand, Abbu?' Sindbad shook his head. She looked at Connor. 'Do you?'

'No,' said Connor, though he thought that perhaps somewhere, in the back of his head, among the tangle there, he understood more than he was admitting. Somehow, some of what Trismagistus was saying was making some kind of sense to him. And he wished that it didn't.

Trismagistus lowered the lantern and placed it on the floor beside the map. He locked the fingers of both hands and pressed his palms together.

'Perhaps you can understand this,' he said. 'If the Tower is not there, then it must have been removed. Erased.' Once again Connor knew those words were aimed at him. 'And if the Tower has been removed, then we are lost.'

They were all stilled by those words. A silence fell upon them. Then Sindbad spoke through the silence.

'You mean here.'

'Yes. The Tower is the way back out of this world to our own. The only way.'

He unlocked his fingers and rested his hands on his knees. His voice when he spoke was softer than ever, the brush of an insect's wing in the air. Yet they heard with utmost clarity every word he said.

'And it is more than that. The Tower is the centre of everything, the living heart of the world. It maintains order, holds all in place. Without the Tower of Truth, the world falls into chaos.'

There flashed into Connor's mind a brief image of himself kicking at the tower his sister had made, saw the books and toys flying through the air. And he saw his own face as he did it, flushed and twisted with anger, rage. He raised his head. Trismagistus was looking at him. Their eyes met. Trismagistus spoke to him.

'It must be restored.'

And Connor knew he must be the one to do it.

'How?' said Sherazhad. 'If we're in here and we can't get out.'

Trismagistus shook his head.

'I don't know.'

Connor kept his eyes on the map. He felt as if

they were all waiting for him to come up with an answer. As if they knew, as he knew, that somehow he was the cause of all that was happening, just as Sherazhad had said he was. And he didn't want to see that knowing in their eyes. So he kept his head lowered, and his eyes fixed on the map. As if studying to find an answer. As if the answer was there.

He became aware again of the humming inside his head. Far off. Perhaps not in his head, then. Perhaps somewhere else.

The map.

'The map,' he said aloud. He was surprised he'd spoken. He hadn't meant to. The words had just come out, as if by themselves, without him thinking about them first. And now he found himself speaking again, just letting the words come, not knowing what they were going to be until he'd spoken them. 'It brought me here . . . the one I found . . . it must have brought you here as well . . . ' He still wasn't looking up, still had his eyes on the map, which seemed to be moving in the light of the moving flame. Waking, stirring, coming to life. He carried on letting the words speak themselves. ' . . . so perhaps this map . . . ' And then he saw what it was, what his eyes had been searching for all this time, without him realizing it. 'There's a city.'

'What?' said Trismagistus. 'Let me see.'

He picked up the lantern and held it over the map. 'I didn't notice it before,' said Connor. 'Here. Look.'

139

It was in the large area of land to the south, the land that Connor had known was a desert when he'd drawn it. And when he'd drawn it, there had been a heap of broken stones there. The ruins of an ancient city, he'd thought then. But now, on this map, the city was no ruin. Within a circular wall, a group of buildings or towers had been drawn, very small and squashed together, but unmistakably a city.

A shadow fell across the map, and Connor looked up to see the pale and bloodless face pushed forward, the lantern above it, gripped by the thin, clawed fingers. The smooth head shone. A cold, eager light burned in the dark sockets. The lips opened and spoke, a single word.

'Ophir.'

And Connor felt the whisper of that word brush across his cheek like a single strand of web.

'Ophir?' said Sherazhad. 'What's that?'

'The name of the city,' said Trismagistus.

'Do you know it?' said Sindbad.

'Oh, yes, I know it,' said Trismagistus. He looked up at them. 'Wide avenues. Tall, shining towers. A city of marvels and wonders. Filled with all the knowledge of the world. If there's a way to the Tower it will be known there.' He jabbed a finger at the map. 'And that is where the map will take us!'

'Will it?' said Sherazhad.

'Yes,' said Trismagistus.

'How?' said Sindbad.

But instead of answering Trismagistus put down the lantern and quickly pushed himself to his feet.

'We must prepare for the journey,' he said. 'We'll need water. And food.' He looked at Connor. 'The bottle,' he said.

'What?' said Connor.

'Fill it. From the barrel.'

Trismagistus turned and went to the corner of the hut where the other barrels were standing and reached down into one of them. Connor picked up the bottle and pushed it beneath the water in the barrel, letting it fill. As he did this, Sherazhad spoke to him in a low voice.

'Do you think he's mad?'

Connor shrugged. 'Maybe,' he said.

'He's talking about going on a journey. Through this map. How is that going to happen?'

The bottle was full. Connor took it out and found the stopper and pushed it into the neck. He wiped his hands dry on his jeans. Sherazhad turned to Sindbad.

'Abbu?'

Sindbad sat thoughtful, silent. He shook his head.

'It happened before,' said Connor.

'But how are we going to make it happen this time?' Sherazhad looked over at Trismagistus. He was taking something out of one of the barrels. She lowered her voice even more.

'I don't trust him. I don't believe anything he says. I think he's a crazy man. Or worse.'

Connor thought she might be right about him being worse. He saw her hand flicker over the handle of her knife. Probably without realizing she was doing it. Sindbad saw it too. He frowned.

Trismagistus came back. He was carrying something in his hands that looked like a number of strips of black leather.

'Here,' he said, and handed a few of the strips to each of them. Connor took his. They were strips of black leather. Old and wrinkled and stiff. He sniffed them. They smelt terrible. Like worn, sweaty shoes.

Sherazhad was pulling a face.

'What's this?' she said. 'You said you were getting some food.'

'This is food,' said Trismagistus. 'Dried meat. It's better than nothing. And there may be nothing where we're going.'

'And where is it we're going again?'

'The city of Ophir.'

'Good. So we just wait for the map to take us.'

'Yes.'

Sherazhad put the strips of dried meat on her lap and folded her arms.

'I'm waiting,' she said.

There was a jolt.

It was as if the hut had been struck a heavy blow that sent them all reeling, falling, tumbling across the floor. At the same time the deep drumming of the whale's heart, and the rush of its blood through its veins grew louder. Connor was knocked sideways and at the same time felt something heavy fall across him that gave a grunt and shoved bony fingers into his face. He pushed and Trismagistus grunted again and rolled off. The lamp had been thrown into a corner and its light guttered upwards. All was shadow beyond.

The drumbeat pounded. The blood roared. There was a loud humming.

Sherazhad was lying on her stomach. She pushed herself up.

'What happened? What's happening?' She looked round, then cried out. 'Abbu!'

Sindbad wasn't there.

Sherazhad scrambled to her feet, staring wildly into the gloom.

'Where is he? Where's he gone?' She swung round fiercely towards Trismagistus. 'What have you done with him?'

There was another jolt, even greater than the first. Connor had just been pushing himself back onto his feet and he was thrown sideways again, colliding with the water barrel and clutching at it as it tumbled with him, spilling water all over him. And the humming grew louder and louder still, a whining, piercing howl, and for a while it was as if he was spinning at the centre of some vast, screaming machine. He kicked the barrel away and at once began to push himself to his feet. He saw Trismagistus on his hands and knees, head thrust forward, eyes and mouth wide, like some beast about to spring. He didn't see Sherazhad. He had to shout above the noise.

'They've gone! Both of them! Is it the map? Is it the map doing this?'

Trismagistus turned his head slowly towards him, and he recoiled in horror. The lantern lay on its side with Trismagistus just above it, and the red light it threw upwards made it appear to Connor as if two blank and eyeless sockets were gaping at him out of a bloody mask. Then there came another heavy jolt, and this time the entire hut rocked over onto its side and Connor was thrown off his feet and went tumbling across the floor as it tipped up and fell onto his back against the wall among the barrels. The lamp went out. Something fell and hit him on the head. He lay on his back in the dark as the hut creaked and groaned and he heard its timbers splintering and he waited for the whole thing to come crashing down about him.

But it didn't. The hut stopped moving, its timbers settled. The humming stopped, all sound. He lay in the stillness and the silence and the darkness. He knew he was alone. But he no longer knew where he was. His hand was touching something. The bottle. His fingers closed around its neck.

And then there came another jolt.

And he gasped at the glare of light and heat.

There was a road stretching out before him, running in a straight line across the desert. It was made of blocks of reddish stone, cracked and broken and buckled with heat and age. The road ran as far as he could see, narrowing in the distance, and then seeming to melt and dissolve in the shimmer of liquid, molten light. It could have been laid a thousand years ago.

There was a movement close by. He turned. Sherazhad stood beside him. She too was looking down the road.

'What is this place?' she said.

'A desert.'

Sindbad was standing just behind her, grinning with the ferocity of the sun upon his face.

'What desert?' said Sherazhad. 'And how did we get here?'

'Through the map.'

They all turned at the sound of Trismagistus's voice. He was standing to the other side of Connor, a little way from the road. His bald head shone in the strong light. He spoke again. 'As I said we would.' He took a step closer to Connor. 'Do you still have it?'

Connor thought about the last time he had seen

the map. It was when they were looking at it on the floor of the hut in the whale's belly. Just before the first jolt. He shook his head.

'No.'

'Pity. But it doesn't really matter. This road will lead us there.'

'Where?' Sindbad too was looking down the road, and grinning with the ferocity of the sun upon his face. 'It seems to go on for ever.'

'But it doesn't,' said Trismagistus. 'It ends at the city of Ophir.'

'And from there we can find the Tower,' said Sindbad.

'That's the plan,' said Trismagistus.

'You have a plan?' said Sherazhad.

Trismagistus smiled.

'Something does,' he said.

Connor looked at him. The intense desert light was making his eyes swim and Trismagistus's face seemed to blur, go in and out of focus. But his words had been clear enough. A plan. Something has a plan. Something making everything happen. But what? And for what reason? He shook his head. It was no good even trying to think about that now. He wanted to be out of this heat.

'Which way do we go?' he said.

'There is only one way,' said Trismagistus. 'Look behind you.'

Connor turned. The others turned. Behind them,

and on either side of the road, nothing but the desert scrubland stretching away into the distance. The road began where their feet stood. They all turned back and looked down the long road, the way they had to go. The heat bounced off it in burning waves. The sky above it a relentless, unforgiving blue.

'We're going to die in this heat,' said Sherazhad.

'My throat's dry already,' said Sindbad.

Suddenly Connor realized that he was holding the bottle in his hand. The clay bottle he had filled with water. He held it up.

'There's water here,' he said.

They passed the bottle round and drank a little from it each in turn. It still had that foul, stale taste, but something about the dryness of the heat, and of their throats, made it a little sweeter. When they'd finished, Connor replaced the stopper.

'We have water, and we have food,' said Trismagistus.

'Food?' said Sherazhad.

'The strips of dried meat I gave you,' he said.

Sherazhad pulled a face. She took one of the blackened strips from a pocket in her trousers and looked at it. 'Oh, yes,' she said. 'I'd have to be starving to try and eat one of these.'

'You may be yet,' said Trismagistus. 'Who knows how far the city is from here?'

'You mean you don't?' said Sindbad.

'Why should I?' said Trismagistus. 'I've never

travelled this road before.' He put his hands to the back of his cloak and lifted a ragged hood that hung there and pulled it over his head. 'We'd better be going,' he said, and set off ahead of them along the road.

Sindbad untied his sash and let his sword drop onto the road, then tied the sash over his head for protection against the sun. He picked up the sword and kept it in his hand.

'My turban would have been better,' he said. 'But this will have to do.'

Sherazhad had also pulled her headscarf over her head. Then she looked at Connor, thought for a moment, and took her knife out of the sash at her waist and untied the sash and held it out to Connor.

'Thanks,' he said.

He reached out and took it and tied the sash over his head.

'Ready?' said Sindbad.

He nodded and looked down the road. Trismagistus seemed already a long way ahead of them, a sketchy, scratchmark figure who might at any moment fade and vanish into the immensity of light.

He set off, and the others with him, along the road through the desert.

They moved through an endless expanse of heat and glare, of hazed and shivered tremblings of light. About them, the desert land of sand and scrub, small bushes of thorn and flowers of flame. Their feet dragged under the sun's weight, and the sky pressed its heat down upon their heads. Every now and then they stopped, and drank from the bottle, just a little, to dampen their cracked lips, ease the parched dryness of their throats. They had to make it last. They didn't know when or if they would come upon fresh water. And each time they stopped the landscape looked the same, as if they had travelled no distance. They did not know how long they had been walking. They had lost all sense of time. So they moved on through the earth's furnace.

Connor and Sherazhad were walking side by side. Sindbad was a little way behind them. Trismagistus was some way ahead.

'How long do you think we've been going?' said Connor. He kept his head down, watching his feet upon the road. He couldn't stand the pain of the light in his eyes when he raised them.

'I don't know,' said Sherazhad. 'It seems like hours, but I can't tell.'

Connor was silent for a while, then he spoke again. 'Do you remember being on the ship?'

'Of course I do,' said Sherazhad.

'When was it?' he said.

'What do you mean?'

'When we were there? How long ago?'

For a while Sherazhad said nothing. When she spoke there was an edge of fear in her voice.

'I don't know that either.'

149

'Neither do I,' said Connor.

He'd been thinking about this for a while now. Trying to put the sequence of events in order, all that had happened since he'd fallen through the map onto the ship. To measure them against each other, work out some sense of time, its length and passage. But he couldn't. It was like trying to measure the things that happen in a dream. In a dream, things appeared to happen in an instant and to go on for ever at the same time. It was like that here. Except this wasn't a dream. In a dream there's a part of you that knows you're dreaming. Here every part of him knew he was awake.

He wanted to say something of that to Sherazhad. And he was trying to find the words to start saying them, when she spoke.

'I'll tell you what I do remember.'

'What?'

'The taste of the dried fruit. Figs and dates. On board the ship. Do you remember that?'

He did. He closed his eyes, thinking about it. He could almost taste the rich sweetness of the fruit, their sweetness in his mouth. He opened his eyes. Sherazhad was looking at him. They smiled at each other.

'Hungry?' she said.

'Yes,' he said.

'We could eat some of that dried meat,' she said.

'Not that hungry,' he said.

They smiled again. Then Sherazhad looked

past him, and the smile left her face, and she said, 'What's that?'

She'd stopped walking and was pointing away to the left of the road. 'There,' she said. 'Look.'

Connor turned and looked.

At first he thought it was just the heat making the air shimmer above the desert. Four or five trembling columns of light some distance from the road's edge. But as he gazed at them they seemed to begin to take on a more solid form. Or it was as if they wanted to take on solid form, and could only do so as long as he looked at them. And he realized that was all he wanted to do, to keep on looking at them. Entranced he watched as delicate spirals of colour appeared and began to coil and wind about those shivering, translucent beings. And at the same time, as if far off, he heard a high, wild singing, as if the voice of light itself.

'They're beautiful,' said Sherazhad. 'Do you see them?'

'Yes,' he said. 'I see them. And they are beautiful.'

'They're calling. They want us to go to them.'

And even as she spoke both he and she were stepping off the road and beginning to walk dreamlike across the sand towards them. The spirals of colour swirled faster, the singing grew clearer, sharper, the figures held out their arms towards them.

'No! Stop! Don't look!'

Sindbad's voice stabbed through the trance, and

Connor felt a strong hand grip his shoulder, pulling him back. He tried to tear himself free of the grip, to run towards those figures waiting for him, but Sindbad's fingers bit deeper into his shoulder so that he cried out in anger, and in pain, and once more that hard, rough voice shouted loud in his ears.

'Look away!'

And he was dragged stumbling backwards, and in that instant the song became a savage snarl of rage, and he caught a glimpse of withered, shrivelled faces glaring at him out of a bloody mist that melted, as the cries melted, into the clear desert light.

He stood on the road again. Sindbad was beside him. Sherazhad was on his other side.

'What were they?' said Connor.

'Djinn,' said Sindbad. 'An evil kind. They eat human souls.'

'But they were so beautiful,' said Sherazhad. 'And their singing.'

'So they would appear to you,' said Sindbad, 'until they had you caught in their embrace. Then you would have seen and heard them differently.'

Connor saw again those withered faces, heard those savage snarls. Despite the heat he shivered.

'You saw something of that,' said Sindbad. Connor nodded. 'Those faces would have been the last thing you saw, those voices the last thing you heard, before they tore your spirits from you and devoured them like jackals.'

'What about our bodies?' said Sherazhad.

'They would have become as theirs are. Things of no substance, desert wanderers, eternally hungry for the souls of others.'

Connor gazed out across the desert, and its vast spaces were no longer empty to his eyes. It was an invisible world, filled with strange figures, of which he had glimpses, and which had almost claimed him for its own.

He turned to Sherazhad. She too looked troubled. They walked on along the road in silence.

At last they came to water.

The desert on either side of the road had been rising steadily, to form a line of rocky bluffs of red sandstone, scarred and cracked by the scourings of sun and wind. Now they came to a place where there was a clump of thorny bushes growing in the shade of the rock, and a group of stunted palm trees. Beneath the trees was a small waterhole. They left the road and made their way to the trees and knelt by the waterhole, scooping up the fresh-tasting water into their mouths. Connor emptied out what remained of the stale water in the bottle and re-filled it from the hole. As he was doing this, Sherazhad said, 'Look!'

He looked up. She was pointing to one of the palm trees. Hanging down from its trunk were a number of long stalks, and at the end of each stalk a large cluster of oval-shaped, reddish-brown fruits. The other trees were hung with the same fruits.

'Dates,' she said. She stood and reached up and plucked one and bit into the soft, sweet flesh, pulling it with her teeth from around the stone at its centre, then sucking at the stone until it was clean. She dropped the stone among the rocks and grinned at Connor.

'Even better than those on the ship,' she said.

She plucked another date and threw it to Connor. He was holding the bottle with one hand and he caught the date with the other, then bit into it, as Sherazhad had done. Its sweetness made his teeth tingle.

'You're right,' he said. He took another bite. 'And definitely better than those strips of dried meat.'

'We may need them yet.'

Trismagistus was crouched over the waterhole, wiping his mouth with the back of his hand. Sindbad shook his head and smiled and stood. He picked a date from a tree beside him.

'We may,' said Sindbad. 'But not tonight at least.'

And as he bit into the fruit he closed his eyes with pleasure.

Then they all plucked more dates from the tree, eating as they picked them until they were full. It wasn't until he started eating that Connor realized just how hungry he'd been. When they'd had enough they sat back against the trees with their stomachs full, though their bodies ached with the weariness of their travels.

The sun was beginning to go down when they arrived there. The sky deepening its blue, a single pale star low on the horizon, the light milder upon the desert stillness. For a while none of them spoke. Sindbad sat with his head back, eyes gazing upwards towards the broad, fronded leaves of the palm trees. Sherazhad's eyes were closed. Trismagistus sat with his head bowed forward, hands resting on his knees. Connor's mind was empty of everything except for that same dull ache that filled his entire body.

After a while, Sindbad looked down and spoke.

'It's lucky we found this place before the sun went down. We'd have frozen in the desert at night. Sleeping against the rocks will give us some warmth.'

'What about tomorrow?' said Sherazhad. 'How long will it take to reach the city?'

She was looking towards Trismagistus. He spoke from beneath his hood.

'I don't know.'

'You said you knew it.'

'I do.'

'You've been there.'

'Yes.'

'Then why don't you know where it is?'

Trismagistus raised his hands to his hood and

155

drew it back a little from his face and looked up at Sherazhad, at all of them. His eyes glittered. The thin, dry voice seemed to come from lips that did not move.

'Because when I was there it was not in this world.'

They all three sat up. It was Sindbad who spoke.

'Where was it?'

'The world I came from.'

'What world is that?' said Sherazhad. 'Your world? What's it like there? Tell us.'

Connor could tell from the sound of her voice she didn't believe what Trismagistus was telling them. But if Trismagistus was aware of that, he showed no sign. He leaned forward a little, and drew his hood further back from his face.

'How can I describe it to you?' he said. 'It's been so long since I left there I hardly remember it myself. It's like a dream to me, half remembered on waking. Fading. An old tale from another age. So it is with your own worlds. Each one unimaginable and strange. This is the only world we have now. The world we share. The only world known to us.' He leaned further forward, his face close to theirs, and his voice was a whisper, and each word as sharp and clear as a blade. 'And this world too, and all that happens in it, all that is happening now, is a story, an old tale. And we are part of its telling.'

Those words cut deep. If they were blades, then

they were blades of ice. Suddenly Connor wanted to see his home again, to see his sister, his mother and father, his friends. He closed his eyes and tried to see them, tried to picture his house, the rooms in his house, himself in those rooms, living his life, his ordinary life. He tried to fix it in his mind, to make it real. But it kept shifting, drifting, smoke in a mirror, and the more he tried to recall it, the further it floated away from him. A dream half-remembered. An old tale. He wanted to cry out. No. No! But the words wouldn't come, his voice made no sound. It was Sherazhad who spoke, and broke the silence.

'What you just said,' she said. 'It doesn't make sense.'

She was staring fiercely at Trismagistus. He smiled at her.

'Tell me something you've come across here that does,' he said. And he pulled his hood across his head and leaned back against the tree.

The sun had almost set now and they felt in the air the first cold of the desert night. Beyond their shelter beneath the bluff, the desert itself was draining of colour, a vast shadowland lit by many stars. While there was light remaining they broke branches from the bushes and gathered them into a pile and the thorns from those bushes they snapped off and placed at the centre of the pile for tinder. This was all on Sindbad's instruction. Then he took Sherazhad's knife and struck it against a stone above the tinder so that the sparks flew among the thorns, and they began to glow, and he bowed his head and blew gently on the glowing thorns until they crackled and sparked themselves. Plumes of tangy smoke rose upwards and small flames flickered and ran the length of the cut branches. So they had a fire for warmth and companionship in the dark.

They sat around the fire, with the heat of the flames on their faces, their hands, letting that heat fold itself into their bodies, so the aching in their limbs became a delicious tiredness, and one by one they eased themselves down beside the rocks or beneath a tree, and the stillness and the silence of the desert night with all its stars lay upon them.

Connor lay on his back looking up at those stars through the fringed leaves of the palm trees and wondered if they were the same as those that shone in the sky in his world. Was this world in a different universe, with its own stars, its own planets? Or was his own world at this moment circling one of those distant stars? He lifted his arm and stretched out his fingers, his hand pressed flat against the dark's fragile skin. Then he slowly closed his fingers, as if he might pluck from the sky his own world, as he had plucked the dates from the tree, shut his hand upon it, hold it safe in his palm. He lowered his arm and held his fist before his face. Then he opened it. It was empty. He turned over on his side and some time after this he fell asleep.

Then he was awake again and it was still night. He didn't know how long he'd slept for, minutes or hours. He lay on his side. Trismagistus was curled in his robe against the foot of the bluff. He was some way off but even so Connor could hear the slow rise and fall of his breathing as he slept. Connor wondered what had woken him and lay there for some moments alert, listening. Then, from somewhere close behind him, he heard Sherazhad speaking softly.

'Abbu.'

'Yes?'

'Those creatures we saw today.'

'The djinn.'

'Are there any others like that here?'

'Yes. And far worse. Marids. Ifreets. Ghouls. Basilisks. Nasnas. All terrible creatures. All things to be feared.'

'How do you know?'

Sindbad was silent for a while. Then he said, 'Everyone who has spent time in the desert knows of them.'

'When did you spend time in the desert? We're pirates, aren't we? We spend all our time at sea. I've never spent any time in the desert.'

Once again Sindbad was silent, and for longer this time. When he spoke again, his voice was deeper, softer, and his words were a conjuring of distant times and places, of visions seen, of trials endured.

'I have stood at the top of high cliffs looking down into a valley filled with serpents and jewels. I have seen the horses of the sea rearing out of the waves and come galloping up the beach with a noise like thunder. The Old Man of the Sea has had me in his grip. Winged men have carried me to the borders of heaven. I have watched whales drinking from streams of amber on the shores of a far island.'

'Where have you seen and done all those things, Abbu?' said Sherazhad.

'In the world I come from.'

'You've remembered them?'

'Yes.'

'Then why don't I?'

There was a puzzlement, and a sadness in Sindbad's voice when he spoke next.

'I don't know, Sherazhad.'

And Sherazhad was silent after that. Connor lay waiting for her to speak, but she didn't. The night was cold and the ground was hard and the stars glittered cold and hard in the sky. They grew brighter as he watched them and came closer or he was rising towards them, and then drifting weightless among those many burning worlds, where there was wonder and terror and things too marvellous to be told, and the worlds themselves too numerous to count.

He woke again and it was early morning. He sat up, then rose to his feet. His back was stiff and he blinked into the already brightening desert light. The others were also waking and rising.

'We ought to start moving,' said Sindbad. 'Before the sun gets too high. Who knows how far we still have to travel?'

He looked at Trismagistus when he said this, but Trismagistus had his hood pulled across his face and made no reply.

They picked more dates from the palm trees and ate them, and then drank from the waterhole, and each took a handful of dates for the journey ahead and then they set off along the road. Connor walked beside Sherazhad but she kept her head bowed and looked at the ground and gave no sign that she even knew he was there. She'd said no word since they'd woken. Sindbad was walking ahead of them and, as on the day before, Trismagistus walked ahead of him, leading the way. Soon the sun was above the horizon and the land once more began to burn.

At last Connor spoke to Sherazhad.

'Do you think we'll ever find this city?'

Sherazhad shrugged.

'I hope it doesn't take too long,' he said. 'I don't think I can stand another day walking in this heat.'

She said nothing. They walked on. Then Connor spoke to her again.

'What if we don't? What if there is no city? You said you didn't trust him. What if he's just making it all up?'

And this time Sherazhad did say something, though she kept her head lowered.

'If he is I'll cut his throat.'

It wasn't just her words that shocked him but the vehemence with which she said them.

'You can't do that,' he said.

Then she looked up at him quickly, and her eyes flashed, and he saw anger there, and hurt.

'Yes I can!' she said. 'Because I'm a pirate and that's what pirates do!'

And she walked ahead of him, and caught up with Sindbad and went on beside him.

So Connor walked on alone, thinking to himself that she wasn't a pirate, after what he'd heard Sindbad say last night he knew she couldn't be, and that she must know this herself. But if she wasn't a pirate, and if she knew nothing of Sindbad's world, then what was she, and where was she from? He saw again the anger and hurt in her eyes, heard the fury in her voice, and realized that she didn't know herself.

Soon the bluffs on either side of the road fell away and what shelter they had given was gone, and the sun was directly above them and sky and land were fused into a single and intense glare of blistering light. They moved on through its heat, scorched and shadowless, and the desert was endless and without horizon. Then they came to a place where huge blocks of broken and shattered stones lay scattered and half buried in the sand and it was here that the road ended.

Alice sat at the table staring at the map. She rubbed her eyes. They were stinging and her head was starting to ache. She liked making stories but she had never made one as long as this before and it was making her tired. She wanted to have a rest. But the Voice wasn't letting her rest. And it kept making things happen that she didn't want to happen. First of all with that man with the horrible face and now with the two pirates. She'd made those pirates and she wanted them to stay pirates but the Voice wouldn't let them. So now they weren't pirates any more and she wasn't sure what they were, especially the girl, and she was getting confused.

She rubbed her eyes again.

Now what?

It was the Voice speaking to her. Alice shook her head.

Something has to happen.

She winced.

What's the matter?

'You're making my head hurt,' she said.

The Voice spoke again, and it was softer.

What's going to happen next?

She shrugged. She didn't know what was going to happen next. She couldn't think.

It can be anything you want, said the Voice.

'Anything?' said Alice.

Yes.

Alice stared at the map. She thought about the desert, about the ruins in the desert. They were there, standing among the ruins. And they were lost.

'I want her to do something brave,' she said.

She can, said the Voice.

'Anything?'

Anything.

'I can choose?'

Yes.

She stared harder at the map. For a moment her eyes blurred and everything shivered and started to break into splinters but then she brought them back into focus. They were standing among the ruins and they were lost. And something was going to happen. Something scary and dangerous. Then she saw it. The sand began to move. Like a wind blowing across it. The sand was moving and something was going to come out of the sand. Then she knew what it was that was going to happen.

'Monsters,' she said.

She couldn't see it, but somehow she knew that the Voice smiled when it spoke.

Monsters.

SIX

The City

They had been walking the road for much of the day. The sun was lower in the sky, though its heat was still fierce, and beat down upon them, and upon the burning, shimmering sand. And now they stood at the road's end. Ahead of them the desert stretched away in all directions. Nothing but sand, and heat, and sky, and light. The thin, black line of the horizon, encircling them like a trap. And here, on either side of that road's end, these broken blocks of stone, like cracked and carious teeth, the tumbled walls and towers of some ancient and long lost city.

Connor wanted to cry, and he wanted to scream, he wanted to run at Trismagistus and beat him with his fists and knock him down and kick him for bringing them here to this lost and empty place. But he was exhausted. He had no strength for anything. He walked over to one of the stones, and then his limbs gave way and he slumped down heavily on the stone and sat, staring at his feet. Then he bent down and grabbed a handful of sand and held it up and let the sand trickle out through his fingers. It made a dry, dead, hopeless sound.

He heard a soft thud and turned to look. Sherazhad was a little way from him, kneeling in the sand, staring ahead. There was a blank look in her eyes.

'Do you want some water?' he said to her.

She looked at him and nodded, and he held the bottle out to her. She took it, drank a little, then handed it back. He took a drink himself and replaced the stopper.

Trismagistus had walked a little way off and was standing among the stones. He lifted the hood from his head and let it fall back. Sindbad was the only one still on the road, and he was watching Trismagistus. At last he spoke.

'So this is your city.'

'Yes,' said Trismagistus. 'Yes. This is it.' He raised his arms, opened them wide. 'Ophir, the magnificent, the eternal city. Its broad avenues, its wide boulevards, its high and shining towers. This is all that remains of it. These fallen, broken stones.' Connor could hear a cracked desperation in his voice. 'The city where . . . ' he said, then his voice faltered and fell silent. His arms dropped to his sides. He too sat on one of those ancient stones. He spoke again, his voice low, but his words carried across that stilled space. 'How many years? Have I been here that long?'

Then Sherazhad stood. She turned to face

Trismagistus. Connor saw the knife gripped in her right hand, hanging at her side. He remembered what she'd said to him earlier that day. Now she spoke to Trismagistus.

'You said the city was in your world.'

'I did. It was. Perhaps it still is. In ruins there too.'

'Then what's it doing here?'

Trismagistus looked up at her.

'What?'

'How can the city, or even its ruins, be in your world, and in this one?' She took a step towards him. 'How did it get here? What's it doing here?'

'What are you doing here?' said Trismagistus. 'Or any of us? How did we get here?' He looked from Sheruzhad, to Sindbad, to Connor. Then he stood. 'It brought us. It wanted us, and brought us here. For its own reasons, not any of our choosing.'

Connor saw how Sherazhad's fingers tightened around the knife-handle. He saw the tension in her wrist and arm, heard it in her voice.

'It?' she said. 'What do you mean, "it"? What are you talking about?'

She took another step towards Trismagistus.

'The Tower,' said Trismagistus.

'The Tower's fallen,' said Sherazhad. 'I heard you say. When we found the map. You said the Tower had fallen. And that it must be rebuilt. And that was why we had to find the city, so we could get to the Tower . . .' Her voice was becoming tighter. Connor

167

could hear it straining in her throat. And he sensed that tightness winding itself through her whole body, and there was a menace in it, and a threat. 'But there is no city,' she said, and took a step. 'It's all ruins.' Another step. 'So how do we get there? How do we get to the Tower?' Another step, and another. 'How we do we get out of this place?'

She was standing just a little way from Trismagistus now, and staring hard at him, waiting for him to answer. And Connor could see the movement in her wrist and she lifted the knife blade. But Trismagistus wasn't even looking at her. He was looking at the broken stones again, and when he spoke there was a sudden wildness in his voice.

'The city,' he said. 'In ruins. And the Tower in ruins.' He wheeled round and stared at Connor and once more Connor felt those eyes stab into him. 'The Tower fell, and the city fell with it.'

And now suddenly the air, lit by the freckled rays of the lowering sun, was lit too with danger. It was in the way Trismagistus was staring at him, in the way Sherazhad's fingers gripped the knife-handle and lifted its blade slowly upwards. In those scattered blocks of tumbled masonry, animating them, as it animated the desert itself with a glittering hostility.

All felt it. All froze.

'What is it?' said Sindbad. 'What's happening?'

There came a hissing of wind, and the sand about them stirred.

Connor felt the wind tug through his hair, slap across his face. Trismagistus's robe, Sindbad's and Sherazhad's loose clothing, flapped in the wind that was growing stronger now, and moaned across the stones, as the sand swirled and coiled and twisted around their feet and was scooped up and flung into their faces. And then the wind was howling and lifting the sand in huge swirls that surged and gusted about them, and Connor was flung backwards by its force, struggling to keep his balance, as the wind battered him, and the flying and whirling sand screamed about him. Suddenly all was dark and the others were lost from his sight. But through his squinting and gritted eyes he saw or thought he saw shadows in the centre of the twisting funnels of sand, thin ribbons of smoke that grew and diminished, faded and reappeared. At first he thought he was imagining them, but the more he gazed on them, the more real they became, elongating, thickening, growing broader, darker. Jags of fire flickered deep within them, that were no longer shadows, but forms and figures with spread wings and bony, claw-footed legs, and reptile faces with opened jaws, whose long, gargling shrieks ripped through the howling wind.

Sindbad's voice came crying out of the storm's centre.

'Ifreets! Sand demons!'

And upon his cry the demons tore free of their

spinning columns of sand, as if called forth by the utterance of their name, nightmare creatures made real in this world, bat-wings beating the sand-clogged air, swooping and diving around and among them, each scream a ragged bolt of flame that cracked and crackled and hissed at their feet.

Connor turned, and ran, and stopped, and turned and ran again, but the demons were everywhere and there was no escape from them. He glimpsed the others running too, this way and that, vague forms glimpsed through the clouds of swirling sand. Trismagistus came towards him, and an ifreet swooped low overhead. He ducked, and flung his hands above his head, then ran on, past him.

There was a flash of flame, and sand hissed up into his face, blinding him for a moment. Then he felt something grab him by the shoulder, claws gripped and biting, and he was picked up off his feet and flung through the howling, sand-whipped air. He came down heavily on his back, a hard thump, the breath jolted out of his body. For a moment he could see nothing, but then there came another terrible screech from close by, and he looked up to see one of the demons standing above him, straddling his body with its thin, backward-jointed, reptile-like legs, its wings beating at the swirling dust, fanged jaws gaping, its arms with their taloned hands spread wide.

Within two narrow slits on either side of its jaws a deep golden light burned.

The ifreet reached down towards him. But something bright flashed above Connor's head, and the creature shrieked in raged pain, and twisted sideways, as dark blood splashed out from a gash across its chest. Then another flash, and a shout, a human shout, and there was Sindbad bringing the blade of his sword round and back above his head to strike again at the wounded demon. But the creature sprang snarling into the air and with a kick from one of its taloned feet sent the sword spinning from his hand. Sindbad gave a cry and stumbled backwards as the demon dropped down on top of him.

Connor rolled over and pushed himself up onto his knees and then back to his feet. Sand swirled thickly around him and for a while he could see nothing, though the choked air was filled with the howling of the demons and lit by garish bursts of flame. Then from close by there came a ragged screech and at the same time a gust of wind tore through and he saw Sindbad thrown onto his back, trying to fend off with his beating fists the crouching demon that straddled him. Then from somewhere else there came a cry and Sherazhad appeared, running towards the demon with her knife in her raised hand. As she drew near she slashed at one of the demon's wings and straightaway it sprang into the air and turned and landed facing her with a scream of rage.

And she froze. She stood with the hand holding the knife outstretched and a look of terror on her face. The demon screamed at her again and her fingers jumped open and the knife dropped into the sand. The demon hissed and took a lurching step towards her and crouched. She didn't move. Connor saw Sindbad struggling to his feet but he knew he would be too late and so he ran forwards and threw himself at Sherazhad just as the demon sprang. He knocked her down and they both fell and the demon leapt over them and was lost in the whirling storm of sand.

A hand grabbed his arm and pulled him to his feet. It was Sindbad. He reached down and pulled Sherazhad to her feet and seemed about to say something when something dark dropped down out of the screaming sand and Sindbad whirled round to face the demon that had landed behind him. Then another shadow lunged down from above and Sherazhad gave a cry as a demon hovering over her knotted its clawed foot in her hair and began to drag her away into the storm. And then there came a scream that tore at his ears and Connor swung round to come face to face with a lizard head whose jaws gaped and whose yellow eyes gazed steadily at him with a malignity that gripped and squeezed his heart. Then a leathery wing swung in and struck him across the face and spun him round and sideways. And he was struck again, a blow to the other side of his head, which spun him back, and round, and he fell forwards heavily, and his face slammed down into the sand. There came a long, ripped-metal shriek of triumph that raked through him and he lay with his fingers digging into the sand and waiting for the horror that he knew would come.

He closed his eyes. And as if from far off he heard a shout.

Then there came a roar of wind followed by another shrieking cry, and it dragged up and away from him, and the air about him was filled with such cries, tatters of sound ripped and flung through the swirling sand. He rolled over and saw the demon that had knocked him down appearing to fall upwards through the sandcloud, its body buckling, convulsing, its solid form crumbling into twists of smoke. And the other demons too were being flung through the air like things of stick and paper and string, and flung so fiercely that they began to come apart. Wings, legs, feet, heads, bodies, voices too, broken and scattered, wreckage blown in the wind, drifts of fluttering ash. And that same wind calming, growing softer, gentler, a desert breeze now, and the air clearing itself of sand, which shivered in little swirls a moment or two, and then was still.

Connor sat up. There was Sherazhad standing close by, blinking in the sudden light. Sindbad too, wiping the sand from his eyes and mouth. A little further off, Trismagistus kneeling, staring about him.

173

There was a livid red gash across the top of his head.

All were still. They were like sleepers awoken. They did not speak.

The air sparkled.

Their injuries were not serious. They were shaken, scratched, cut, bruised, but no real hurt had been done. Connor had grazes down each side of his face where the ifreet's wings had struck him. There were several scratches along Sherazhad's forehead. Sindbad's right hand was cut where the demon had clawed at it. The worst wound had been that received by Trismagistus, that gash across the top of his head. It had bled down his face, streaking his white skin with red, which he had wiped and smudged with the sleeve of his robe. Now he had pulled his hood across his head to cover the wound.

They sat each of them on one of the old stones in a desert that was beginning to darken, whose sky once more was beginning to show its stars. Connor sat near to Sherazhad. She leaned forward, her head bowed. Sindbad and Trismagistus were talking about what had happened. Sindbad had retrieved his sword and it hung at his side.

'They seemed to come from nowhere,' he was saying. 'And then vanished into nowhere again.'

Trismagistus looked towards those few pale stars glimmering near the horizon.

174

'They were called,' he said.

'What do you mean?' said Sindbad.

'Called here,' said Trismagistus. 'Then called away.'

'By what?'

Trismagistus gave a sidelong glance at Sindbad, but said nothing.

'The Tower,' said Sindbad.

Trismagistus smiled.

'But you said the Tower was destroyed.'

'It is.'

'Then how can it have called those demons?'

Once more Trismagistus looked towards the horizon. It was dark out there now, a line of hazed shadow crumbling upwards into the sky.

'The Tower is only a shell. It encloses what lies within. A force, a power, an energy. A mind perhaps. A spirit. It is that which shapes this world, causes all to happen within it. It called you and the girl here. It called the boy. As once, long ago, it called me.' And now he turned his head to look once more at Sindbad. 'And if the Tower is destroyed, it must be working through something else. Some temporary dwelling place. Guiding us to the ruins of the Tower, so that it can be remade, its home restored.'

'Then why did it call the demons? Why is it making things so difficult for us?'

Trismagistus smiled again, a thin, tight, bitter smile.

'It likes to play.'

Connor had been watching Trismagistus, listening to him, but now he looked away. Over to the west the sun was huge, low on the horizon. Although Trismagistus had been speaking to Sindbad, Connor had felt that the words were meant for him, and him alone. And he was beginning to understand what he meant. He was remembering the stories his sister made up, those winding, meandering stories where anything could happen, just because she wanted it to. What was happening to them seemed to Connor to be like one of those stories. Except that he was in this story, that it not only felt, but was real. A story coming to life as he moved through it. As the map had seemed to come to life as he had drawn it, at home, on the ship. His fingers making marks on the paper. His sister making words in the air. He remembered the shout he had heard just before the demons were called away. From somewhere far off. As if not in this world.

Something flashed in the sand, catching the sun's dying light. He stood and went across to it. It was Sherazhad's knife. He picked it up and stood looking at it for a while. Then he walked across to Sherazhad and held the knife out to her.

'Here,' he said.

Sherazhad looked up at the knife.

'I don't want it,' she said.

'Why not?'

'I dropped it.'

'And I've just picked it up.'

'You can keep it, then.'

Her voice was sullen. She looked away. He stood there holding the knife, and feeling stupid, and annoyed because she was making him feel stupid.

'It's your knife,' he said.

She turned to him sharply again, and snapped at him.

'Not any more. What do I want with it? I dropped it. I was scared and I dropped it.'

'I was scared too,' said Connor. 'We were all scared.'

'It's not the same thing!' said Sherazhad. 'I'm not supposed to be scared. I'm supposed to be . . . ' She stopped. Her voice was beginning to break, and there was something breaking inside her too, that she was trying to hold together. And she breathed in deeply and held it together, and then carried on speaking, slowly, deliberately. 'I'm supposed to be brave. The terror of the eastern seas. The pirate captain's fearless daughter. But I'm not. I'm not fearless. Sindbad isn't a pirate captain. I'm not his daughter. It was all just made up.'

'Why did you make it up?' said Connor.

'I didn't,' said Sherazhad. 'It was there in my head. I thought it was true. Now I know it's not. And I don't know who or what I am.' Then the old fierceness flashed again in her dark eyes as she glared at him and her voice was trembling. 'Was it you? Did you make it all up? All this? Is it you?'

He thought about it. Then he said, 'I don't know.'

She turned away from him. He looked down at the knife in his hand. He was holding it with the blade inwards, the handle extended towards Shera-zhad. Now he turned it round so that he held it with blade out and down.

'But I'm going to try and do something to help us,' he said.

He took a few steps towards Sindbad and Tris-magistus and stood facing them. The setting sun was behind him and it cast his shadow long and thin and dark across the sand, the broken blocks of stone. They looked up at him.

'When I was drawing the map,' he said, 'I could feel it coming alive. The same thing happened when I started to draw the one on the ship. So perhaps if I draw the city that will come alive too.'

Trismagistus sat up. With the evening's dying light his face was in darkness beneath the hood. But Connor could feel his eyes staring at him out of that darkness. Yet Trismagistus said nothing and it was Sindbad who spoke.

'What will you draw it with?'

Connor held up the knife blade.

'This.'

And now Trismagistus spoke and his voice had

the same dry and granulated sound as the wind that had hissed through the sand a little while before.

'Can you remember what it looks like?'

'Yes,' said Connor. 'There was a round wall and towers inside it.'

Trismagistus nodded.

'Try it,' he said.

Connor went towards a large flat-topped block of stone and knelt in front of it. Sindbad and Trismagistus stood and watched him. From where she stood Sherazhad watched as well. He closed his eyes for a moment and fixed there the image of the city as he had seen it on the map they had found inside the bottle. Then he opened his eyes and placed the point of the knife against the flat top of the stone and began to draw.

There was little light to see by and he had to bend his face close to the stone as he dragged the knife-point across its surface and cut a wide circle there. It made a dry scraping sound and he felt the vibration of it tingle through his fingers and hand. But it was when he began to inscribe the straight lines of the towers within the circle that he realized that the tingling was more than just from the movement of the blade across the stone. It began to run through his whole body, and was in the air as well, and in the ground, as if the whole darkening landscape was suddenly charged and crackling with electricity. And as he was scratching the downward stroke of the final line a spark leapt from the knife's point and the knife itself sprang from his hand and spun in the air. Its blade glittered in the evening light and gave off a high-pitched singing note which seemed to strike the stone in front of Connor, and the stone took up the note, which jumped through the air from one stone to the next so that now all the tumbled broken stones were singing.

Connor sat up and back and got quickly to his feet. He stood with the others while all about them the stones sang that high-pitched note and began to shiver with it. Then the note struck downwards through the earth and was answered from far below by another note, deep and resonant, and they felt it vibrating through their footsoles and felt the ground vibrating with it. Then it was as if some explosion had taken place in the earth's bedrock and its shockwave thumped upwards making the ground buckle and shake and then another shockwave came, and another and another, each one with increasing force until they were thrown off their feet and fell clinging to the ground that heaved and rolled under them like the piling waves of a storm-split ocean. And now with a grinding, thunderous roar the stones about them thrust upwards out of the sand, rising higher and higher, and wide flat slabs of stone reared up beneath them. For some moments it went on until at last all movement and vibration ceased and the echo of the roar faded and died and they lay with shut eyes and all about them was stillness and silence.

They opened their eyes and slowly rose to their feet. And then gazed with wonder at where they stood. Beneath their feet was a wide avenue of stone. On either side of the avenue towers of smooth and polished stone which reached away along the avenue as far as they could see. It was almost night. A full moon was rising. Its light caught the edges and surfaces and tops of those towers, and splashed upon the surface of the stone avenue. And to their amazed eyes all was glitter and lustre and shine in the city of Ophir.

Alice blinked and looked up. Somebody had spoken and it wasn't the Voice. Her mother stood in the doorway.

'Alice?'

Alice didn't say anything. She just smiled. Her mother spoke to her again.

'I said are you all right?'

'Yes,' said Alice.

'I thought I heard you shout.'

Alice kept on smiling.

'I did,' she said. 'It was part of my story.'

'You're making up a story?'

Alice nodded. Her mother looked at the toys and books piled around her where she sat on the rug and frowned but she didn't say anything about that. She turned her head and looked towards the table and frowned even more.

'Where's Connor?'

'I don't know,' said Alice.

'I thought he was in here with you.'

'He must have gone out.'

'Don't you know where he went?'

Alice shook her head. Her mother carried on looking at the table.

'He said he had some homework to do. Drawing a map of some kind, I think he said.'

'He was, yes,' said Alice. 'He finished it. Then he went out.'

Now her mother walked across to the table.

'Is this it?'

She stood there looking down at the map.

'I thought you said he'd finished it.'

'He has.'

'It doesn't look finished to me. He's scribbled over something. Do you know anything about it?'

Alice didn't say anything. Her mother looked up.

'Alice?'

'No,' said Alice.

Her mother glanced at the map again.

'I hope he's going to put it right,' she said. 'He can't give it in looking like that. It's a shame. It spoils it. The rest of it looks very good. Very . . .'

She stopped speaking and lowered her hand and placed the tips of her fingers on the paper. And for some moments she stayed like that looking down at the bridge her fingers made pressed against the map, and Alice began to be afraid and she sat up, and she spoke in her head to the Voice because she knew it was listening.

No, she said. No, don't.

Then a shiver seemed to run along her mother's back and she took her fingers off the map and looked up and across at Alice. She had a puzzled look on her face now as if she was trying to remember something but then the puzzled look went away and she smiled when she spoke.

'Well . . . yes . . . I suppose he will put it right . . . '

'He will,' said Alice.

Then Alice's mother was her mother again and she walked briskly from the table to the door and opened it and turned and stood in the doorway.

'Where did you say he'd gone?'

'I didn't,' said Alice.

'Oh,' said her mother. Then she said, 'He'll be at Peter's. Tell me when he comes back.'

'I will,' said Alice. And then as her mother turned again to go out through the doorway, she said to her, 'Have you done my room yet?'

Her mother looked at her from over her shoulder.

'I've only just done Connor's,' she said. 'I'm just about to make a start on yours. And by the state of it I think I'll be on it for the rest of the day.' She nodded towards the toys and books on the floor. 'Make sure you tidy those up when you've finished.' And then she was gone and the door swung shut behind her.

Then Alice wanted to jump to her feet and run after her and ask her could she help to tidy her room? She just wanted to be with her mother and doing ordinary things, she wanted to be away from the living room and the map and the broken tower and the story. She would go upstairs with her mother and they would tidy her bedroom together and when they'd finished Alice would come back downstairs and Connor would be back and the Voice would be gone.

In fact she did stand up. But as soon as she did the Voice spoke.

Where are you going?

She didn't need to answer. The Voice knew.

You can't leave, it said. You have to stay. We have to finish the story.

Alice wasn't sure she wanted to finish the story. It was becoming too frightening, and too real. Those monsters. It had been as if they were in the room with her. She'd had to shout out loud to make them go away.

But they went away, said the Voice. You made them. And you can make the story finish as well.

'So that everything turns out all right?' she said.

Everything will turn out as it should, said the Voice.

Alice knew that wasn't the same thing. But she knew as well that she had to carry on.

That's right, said the Voice. Now sit.

Alice sat. She took a breath then closed her eyes.

And it was night and the moon was shining and they were in the city.

They walked along one avenue and then another, sometimes coming to a corner, sometimes a cross-roads, turning to the right or to the left, and on either side of them along every avenue rose the towered buildings of the city, some flat-topped, others tapering to a point. All had steps or smooth ramps of stone winding around the outside towards the top. All stood silent and shining in the moon's full light. Silent and shining and empty. Their edges and surfaces seeming to tremble as if woven from some delicate silken thread.

An unreal city, a dream city.

Trismagistus led the way. He walked without hesitation, and spoke to them sometimes of Ophir and its wonders.

'It was a city of scholars,' he said. 'Of the learned and the wise. They gazed into the heart of things and all things became known to them. All that can be known. Great secrets that are lost now and shall never be known again. For the city itself has long fallen and been lost to its world. What you see is the memory of the city, its outward form.' And he turned now to look at Connor. 'Set here by your hand. But see what a fragile hold it has on this world. Who knows how long it will remain here? Long enough I hope for us to find what we need.'

He didn't say what that was and hurried on around another corner and into yet another wide avenue.

Connor went on a little behind him. Then he was aware of Sherazhad walking beside him. She spoke to him in a low, accusing voice.

'I said it was you all along. Right at the start on the ship. I said it was you making everything happen.'

Connor replied without looking at her.

'If I did, I didn't mean to.'

'It doesn't make any difference,' she said. 'It comes to the same thing.'

Then she dropped back and he walked on alone. His head was bowed. His thoughts buzzed and hummed like swarming insects in his brain.

He had drawn the map and the Tower on the map.

The Tower controlled everything in this world. Made things happen.

No, not the Tower. The thing inside the Tower. Whatever that was.

A force, an energy. What kind of thing was that? Was it living? Did it have a shape?

But the Tower was destroyed, and this thing was out. Working through something else.

Someone else.

Who?

Making everything happen.

Me?

Like a story.

Who?

Like one of his sister's stories.

Like?

Or was it not like?

But . . . ?

He heard her voice.

' . . . *far, far away to another country, and you might never come back again. And there's lots of magical things in that other country, and frightening things as well, monsters and giants, all kinds of horrible creatures . . .* '

One of his sister's stories.

She'd scribbled out his drawing of the Tower.

He'd kicked over the Tower she'd made.

The two of them together.

His fingers making marks on the paper. His sister making words in the air.

And her voice he'd heard shout to get rid of the demons.

'We're there.'

He looked up quickly. Trismagistus had spoken and was standing now at the end of the avenue, where it opened onto a wide square courtyard filled with the moon's light. Connor approached. Sherazhad and Sindbad stood beside him. In the centre of the square stood a large building. It was of the same white stone as the towers that surrounded it, great square blocks hewn and smoothed and fitted almost seamlessly together. Its roof was a huge dome. In the wall facing them steps led up to a raised walkway that ran the length of the wall and around the sides of the building, and a little way along this was a low wooden door. The moon stood directly above and the whole building gleamed with the full wash of its light. And there was a stillness and a solidity about it that made it appear somehow more real than any of the towers that rose above it. As if whatever reality the city had was owed entirely to this one building.

They gazed at it in silence for some moments. Then Sherazhad spoke.

'What is it?'

'The centre of the city,' said Trismagistus. 'The living heart of Ophir.'

'Will it lead us to the Tower?' said Connor.

'What it contains will lead us there,' said Trismagistus.

'And what does it contain?' said Sindbad.

'The knowledge of all the worlds,' said Trismagistus, and he set off across the square towards the building.

'So we have to follow him again,' said Sherazhad.

'It seems so,' said Sindbad.

'But not trust him,' said Sherazhad. 'I'll never trust him.' She glanced at Connor when she said that, as if she didn't trust him either, and he was hurt by it, though he thought he knew why she didn't, but could think of nothing he might say to make her feel differently.

They followed Trismagistus across the square to the building. The moonlit silence, the quietude of stone. A domed sky star-spangled. No movement but theirs in that whole dreamlike and dreaming city.

They climbed the steps and stood before the door. A bolted iron ring in its wooden panel.

'What if it's locked?' said Sherazhad.

Trismagistus took hold of the iron ring and lifted it and turned it slowly to the right. There was the metal click and rattle of a latch lifting. He turned to Sherazhad and smiled, thin-lipped, humourless. Then he placed his fingers against the door and pushed. There was a faint creak of wood and the door swung open. Trismagistus bowed his head and stood for a moment in the doorway, gazing inwards. Connor could see only darkness beyond. Then Trismagistus went forward into that darkness and Connor and the others went through after him. The door closed itself behind them.

Moonlight filled the chamber in which they stood, flooding in through a circular opening in the domed roof above. It was vast and many sided, and

189

its walls were panelled with a dark, reddish coloured wood, and from floor to ceiling each panelled wall was stacked with shelves of books.

Trismagistus spoke.

'The great library of Ophir,' he said.

Sherazhad gave a sharp intake of breath.

'And who are they?' she said.

Connor turned to her. She was not looking at the books but upwards towards the domed roof. He followed her gaze and what he saw made him start in surprise. There were figures painted all around the surface of the dome, tall, lean figures, dressed in robes similar to the one Trismagistus wore, men with bearded and solemn faces, unsmiling and austere. But what struck Connor most about them were their eyes, large and dark and oval-shaped, that gazed with a fierce intensity into unmeasured distances, as if contemplating the innermost workings of this world and all the worlds beyond.

Trismagistus spoke, the scratch of his voice like an autumn leaf blown across the tiled floor.

'The citizen scholars of the city. All that remains of them. These painted figures. And their books.'

'So many books,' said Sindbad.

'There must be thousands,' said Connor.

'A thousand and one,' said Sherazhad.

Connor turned to her.

'More than that.'

'She means they are beyond counting,' said Trismagistus. 'An infinite number of books. Yes?'

'Yes,' said Sherazhad.

'They can't be infinite,' said Connor. 'There has to be a certain number.'

'Do you want to try counting them?' said Sherazhad.

Connor looked at the books ranged around the walls of the chamber, crammed together on the shelves.

'No,' he said.

Trismagistus stepped away from them, walked to the centre of the chamber, stood there. And he appeared to them unreal in that lit moment, some wraith spirit woven from the moon's webbed light.

'I was a scholar such as these,' he said. 'A young novitiate, longing to be as they were, to be numbered and revered among the wise. To be more than they were. The wisest, the best. Days and nights I passed here in study, seeking knowledge, understanding. And it was here that the book came into my hands that changed my life for ever. That set me on the path I still follow. That opened the door to a world of wonders. And terrors. The book that leads the way to the Tower of Truth.'

'And that book is here?' said Sindbad.

'It is.'

'Where?'

Trismagistus raised his arms, spread them wide.

'We have to look through all these?' said Shera-zhad. 'It's impossible.'

There came to Connor's mind the image of a bookshelf, of a book falling off that shelf onto the floor and he was speaking even before he realized it.

'The book will find us.'

'No.' Trismagistus dropped his arms and stared hard at Connor. 'It will find you.' He took a few steps forward and stopped. 'Or rather, you will find it.'

'Me?'

And now Sherazhad and Sindbad were staring at him as well.

'How?' he said. 'I can't find it.' He looked at them, looking at him. 'There are too many.' From one to the other, their eyes on him. 'It could be anywhere. It's impossible. Like you said. I don't even know what it looks like. Why should it have to be me?'

Trismagistus came back across the chamber, the hem of his robe making a soft swish across the tiled floor. He stood in front of Connor.

'Because it does,' he said simply. 'Now begin.'

'Begin what?' said Connor. 'I don't know what to do!'

'Look,' said Trismagistus.

He raised his hand, motioned it towards the centre of the chamber where he himself had stood a few moments before. Then stood waiting. And Shera-zhad and Sindbad stood waiting. He looked towards the centre of the chamber where the moonlight fell

192

in a wide pool. With the painted faces of the scholars above. His stomach tightened, a shiver ran beneath his skin. But there was nothing else to be done. He walked towards the centre and took his place.

And stood there. And stood. Long minutes passed, one dragging by after another. Silence in that vast moonlit chamber. His own throat dry, his heart thudding against his chest. He looked up towards the dome, saw scholars there, their dark and stippled eyes seeming now to be fixed on him. As if they too were waiting for him to act. To do something. To find the book.

He closed his eyes. He could feel the moonlight on his shut lids. It spangled in the back dark of his head. Little bright flashes of spiked ice. Moving, dancing. Far stars in the distant sky. And somewhere in those vast distances the humming began. Heard first when he had begun drawing the map, perhaps the voice of the map itself calling to him. Now calling again and growing louder as it called, deep and low and thrumming, both within him and without, reverberating around the vast domed chamber, one voice and many. He saw the moonlight rippling about, saw the walls of the chamber tremble, shiver, felt the pressure of the droning note building inside him, pushing against the walls of his skull. It felt as if something was drilling hard against the bone and a high-pitched whining scream rose out of the humming that set his teeth on edge, his root nerves jangling, and he wanted to cry out, and he was going to cry out, but at that moment of greatest pressure and bite and strain something gave like a catch being released, and the screaming and the humming stopped suddenly and in the shock and jolt of that release his eyes snapped open. And he was watching a book falling from one of the upper shelves.

It descended slowly through the moon-stippled shadows, floating, spiralling downwards like some strange bird with wings outspread and turning on the wind's updraught. But here there was no wind, and they were no wings but pages that fluttered with a dry whisper and closed as the book revolved and righted and came to rest soundlessly on the tiled floor.

Connor and the others crossed to stand around, above the book. It was large and heavy looking, its cover shabby and frayed and torn along the edges, its spine cracked. A stale, musty smell rose to their nostrils. It looked as if it would fall apart the moment a hand was laid upon it. Yet Trismagistus did reach down and lift the book and held it between his hands and brushed the palm of one hand across the cover. Connor saw that there was no title there or writing of any kind.

Without speaking Trismagistus turned and made his way quickly across the chamber towards one of the panelled walls. They followed him.

'I suppose it's the book we're looking for,' said Sherazhad.

'I suppose it is,' said Connor.

'And you made it fall,' she said.

'I must have done,' said Connor.

'How?'

He looked at her.

'I don't know,' he said. Then he said, 'When I was standing there, did you hear anything?'

Sherazhad shook her head.

'No,' she said. She looked at Sindbad. 'Did you?'

'I heard nothing,' said Sindbad.

By this time they had come to the wall where Trismagistus stood with the book. As with the other walls it was lined with books reaching to the ceiling. In front of it stood a high, sloped wooden desk. Connor glanced to right and left and saw similar looking desks at the shelves there. Trismagistus placed the book on the desk and made as if to open it. Then he stopped and turned to Connor.

'Open it,' he said.

Connor stepped forward to the desk. Its top was on a level with his head but he noticed a narrow platform jutting out from between the legs of the desk just above the floor, some kind of foot-rest perhaps, and he stood on this so that he was raised above the desk. Then he took hold of the front cover between finger and thumb and opened it. It took him a few seconds to realize what he was looking at, and then he gave a gasp of recognition and surprise.

It was the map.

Or rather it was part of the map, an enlarged section of it, showing an undulating edge of coast-line running across the page from the top left to the bottom right corner and to the right of it two rough drawings of trees, each with a quick down-ward stroke for the trunk and thinner lines sketched on either side for the branches. Connor remembered drawing that coastline and trees like those himself. Now here it was, greatly magnified, on the first page of the book. On the next two pages were more sec-tions of the same coastline, which he recognized as that of the large northern country, and so on for many more pages, and not just the coastline but its whole interior. The entire country must have cov-ered about thirty pages, and that was only a small fraction of the total number of pages.

He turned the next page and Sherazhad gave a cry.

'Our ship!' She looked up at Sindbad. 'It is, isn't it?'

Sindbad nodded, and he gave a faint smile.

'Yes,' he said. 'It is.'

The prow was drawn in two sections over a dou-ble page. The rest of the ship was drawn over the following eight pages. And in further pages were drawn the flukes of the whale, the desert land, and the city of Ophir itself, its towered and ramped buildings within its circular wall, the wide avenue leading to the central square, and in the centre of that a detailed drawing of the library in which they now stood. And that building and the city in which they stood he himself had scratched upon stone not long ago and made appear. He shook that strangeness from his head and looked up. There were Trismagistus to one side and Sindbad and Sherazhad to the other leaning over him.

'It's all here, isn't it?' said Connor. 'The whole map.'

Trismagistus's eyes flashed cold flame. His breath blew dry across Connor's face when he spoke.

'It is. As I first saw it all that time ago. Turning the pages as you are doing now. Sensing the wonder of that other world that had fallen into my hands. Knowing that there was a purpose behind it. So I made a copy, as you did. Drawing rough sketches onto scraps of paper at first, piecing those scraps together, then making a fair copy onto a single sheet, until at last the map was made.'

'You drew the map?' said Connor.

'Yes,' said Trismagistus.

'Which one?'

Trismagistus leaned in closer. The domed shadow of his head fell across the book. His words were soft sprinklings of dust upon its pages. It was as if Sindbad and Sherazhad had dissolved into the shadows and there were only these two alone in the chamber, in the city, in that entire world.

'There is only one map. And there is only one maker of the map. It is that which called to me, took possession of me, urged me on. That which called to you also, guided your hand across the paper. That single, indivisible power which calls to us both now.'

All Connor could see now was the pale face hanging over his, the deep pits of the eyes, their cold light burning more fiercely than ever. He sensed a craving, a hunger in those eyes and the soul that raged behind them.

'The Tower,' said Connor.

A hand gripped his shoulder.

'The Tower. It's why we are here. What we are here for.'

A thin finger jabbed clawlike at the book, the thin voice hissed. 'Turn the pages. Find it!'

Connor turned the remaining pages one after the other. As he drew near to the end he saw the contours of that island in the far north taking shape until at last it was complete, and only one page remained. He turned it. And on that final page was the Tower.

A thrill of excitement rushed through Connor's veins, shivered beneath his skin. This was the tower that he had drawn on the paper in his living room at home. He recognized the contours of its shape, the flow of the line, the cracked lines across its surface.

It was his Tower, and it was real, and he was filled with a sudden longing to find it and take possession of it.

But there was something else on the paper besides the Tower. A line of strangely shaped symbols running along the bottom of the page, angles and curves and whorls, like the letters of some ancient and forgotten language. And with another thrilled rush he realized that was just what they were. He was about to turn to Trismagistus and ask him about them when suddenly the fingers that had been gripping his shoulder dug in hard and deep and he gave a cry of pain and then he was pulled away sharply from the desk and found himself stumbling against Sindbad as Trismagistus pushed forward and picked up the book and turned to face them with it held out before him.

Shocked by the suddenness of his action the three stared at him as his lips began to move and from his mouth issued sounds none of them had heard before, rasping gutturals of speech, a cracked and ragged language that in its very sound filled them all with horror. And then he finished speaking and a smile of triumph and exaltation twisted across his face, and that look was the last thing they saw of him in that place.

The book thumped heavily onto the floor and he was gone.

SEVEN

The Tower

They stared at the space where Trismagistus had stood, at the book lying open on the floor where it had dropped from his hands. For a moment they were all too stunned to speak or move. It was silent in the chamber and growing darker.

At last Sherazhad spoke.

'What happened?' she said. 'Where is he? Where's he gone?'

'To the Tower, I think,' said Sindbad. 'As he meant to all along.'

'I said I didn't trust him.' Sherazhad's voice rose and the indignation and anger in it rang throughout the chamber. 'All along I said it.' And then she swung round to Connor. 'And you! You helped him!'

She glared at him, her eyes blazing, as if challenging him to deny her accusation. And he couldn't. Because he knew that in some way she was right, and that he had played his part, however unwittingly, in helping Trismagistus to betray and abandon them. So he simply stared back at her and tried to hold her gaze and said nothing. But he couldn't, so he turned away, and walked over to where the book lay on the floor.

He stood above it looking down. Behind him he could hear Sherazhad and Sindbad talking and it was as if their voices were coming to him from across a great void, broken and fragmentary echoes of sound.

'No time. Arguing. Do something.'

'What? Do?'

'Something. Try.'

There was a pulse throbbing in his head. It beat against the inside of his skull and behind his eyes, a soft-edged red glow thrumming slowly. It made it hard to focus on the book, which itself seemed to be lying beneath a pool of water whose surface rippled with shadow and light. So too those distant voices, rippling, pulsating.

'Nothing we can . . . '

'He will . . . '

'Nowhere to go . . . '

'The boy . . . '

'Lost . . . '

'Do something . . . '

Do something. That was it. That's why he'd come over here. To do something. What was it? He tried to think but the pulsing in his head was growing more insistent and the book seemed to be sinking deeper into the ripples of the pool, or melting into them. The book. Yes. He had to pick up the book. That should be easy. He squatted down and reached out and pushed his hands through the throbbing and pulsating waves of red light and they seemed to go a long way before his fingers at last clamped onto the edges of the book and he lifted it up and stood. He'd done it. He'd done something. Now what?

A voice, a single word floated across to him.

'Look.'

That's what he was doing. He was looking. The book lay in his hands and he was looking at it. And something in the book was looking at him.

The Tower.

It stood on the page and it was looking at him.

Two eyes staring at him.

And a face.

A face like a cracked mask with a twisted smile.

And in its two eyes a cold light burning.

He recoiled from the horror of it.

And a voice spoke and it was his sister's voice.

There was a horrible face. Looking out of the window. It frightened me and I wanted to get rid of it.

Get rid of it. Get rid of that face. That cracked and twisted mask staring at him out of the window in the Tower. Tear it off, stamp on it, smash it to pieces.

He knew now why his sister had scratched out that face.

He took hold of the page and tore it out.

And as the page came away in his hand the sound of its tearing reverberated throughout the chamber, rebounding from wall to wall, and amplified so that it sounded as if the walls themselves were being torn from their foundations.

The edges of the Tower shivered, as if struck.

There came a cry of triumph and exultation.

There came a long cry of hopelessness and despair.

There came a cry of rage and fury and it came from his own throat.

He tore the page, he tore the Tower, into pieces, and flung the pieces to the floor.

The chamber shook.

There was a crash.

'What was that?'

'What's happening?'

'What have you done?'

He looked up.

Sherazhad stood facing him and the expression on her face was a mixture of fury and terror. Sindbad was turned away, staring up at the walls, the roof of the chamber. There came another blow and shockwave, as if the chamber had been struck from outside by some giant hand, and a book fell from one of the shelves and crashed to the floor. And then another fell, and another, and another. And then there came another mighty jolt and all the books and their shelves with them were tumbling and crashing to the floor.

Sindbad swung round.

'We have to get out,' he said. 'The whole place is coming down.'

As if in confirmation there came the deep grinding noise of stone shifting against stone, followed by an echoing boom that once more shook the chamber, and then they were all three running, stumbling across the floor towards the door in the far wall as shelves and books continued to rain down upon and around them. But before they had reached halfway there came another grinding boom and the floor buckled inwards and split wide and a ragged hole opened up at their feet.

'Get back,' shouted Sindbad, but even as he did the floor crunched and heaved and he toppled forward into the hole. Sherazhad gave a cry and reached out for him, but it was too late, and then she was standing teetering on the edge, trying to keep her balance, her arms waving above her head. Then she gave a half twist and Connor saw her face for a moment and its look of sheer terror and then her body twisted round again and she was scrabbling at the air and then tumbled forward and she was gone.

The chamber lurched and Connor was pitched onto his hands and knees. Stones were falling now and with a splintering crash the domed roof shattered and the broken figures of the scholars came crashing down. The floor lurched and groaned and another grinding crack opened the hole wider, and at the same time Connor was thrown onto his stomach and went sliding towards it. He grabbed at the side of the hole and clung to it with both hands, hanging halfway over, looking down. There was nothing but darkness below and no thought in his head, and he lay there gazing into the darkness when he felt the edges he was holding on to give and the floor dropped away beneath it and he dropped with it.

But it was no sheer drop into nothingness.

He fell a short way and then his shoulder and left arm hit a rock floor and then his left hip and leg. The fall jolted through his body and he gasped with the shock of it and he lay still for some moments getting his breath back. He could feel rock on either side of him and the uneven rock floor he was lying on sloped downwards a little, with his head towards the slope. Once he was breathing more easily he managed to ease himself onto his front and then by pushing against the floor with his hands and pulling his knees up at the same time he manoeuvred himself into a sitting position.

He was in total darkness. He looked up but there was darkness above too and no sign of the hole he had fallen through. There was no sound. He spoke into the darkness.

'Sindbad? Sherazhad?'

The sound of his voice had a deadened, muffled quality. He listened for a reply. There was none. He spoke again, louder, but there was still that same

dead sound and still no reply. As if he was completely alone. As if both Sindbad and Sherazhad
had just vanished. Unless there was a way out of this
place. Perhaps a passage leading off. Or perhaps he
was already in a passage. He decided to find out.
There was nothing else he could do.

But moving was difficult. The rock walls on either
side of him pressed against his shoulders, making
it impossible for him to stand or even crawl on all
fours. He just didn't have the room to move. So he
began to slide himself along the rock floor, pulling
his legs up and pushing them out again as he pushed
against the walls with the flat of his hands. He went
on like this for some time and then he noticed that
the walls were gradually moving further apart while
at the same time the floor sloped more steeply. He
stopped and thought what to do. He could try getting on to his hands and knees now, perhaps stand.
But that didn't feel safe to him. He didn't know
what else might be down here, what he might come
across further along the passage. Creatures of some
kind, ancient cave dwellers. Pale, colourless, sight-
less things, with shells and many legs, or no shells,
and jellied, footless bodies. He would rather encounter something like that with his feet than with his
hands. He continued shuffling along the passage.

But now it was sloping even more steeply and
he was having to press his hands firmly against the
wall to prevent himself from sliding forward. He

could feel the angle of the passage dragging at him and the strain of pushing against it, of resisting the force of that downward momentum, was making his arms, his whole body, ache. And it was becoming too much for him. His heart began to beat faster and he could feel a panic tightening in his stomach as he kicked with his heels against the forward, downward drag. His hands slipped from the walls and he made a grab at them, and skinned his knuckles, and then twisted his body sideways and made another grab at one wall with both hands. His fingers scrabbled at the rock and his legs kicked out and then he was sliding helplessly down the steepening slope of the passage and it felt as if the whole weight of rock and the world above was piling on top of him and thrusting him down.

Then he realized that he could see. A faint light was illuminating the walls and floor of the passage down which he was sliding, and it was growing steadily brighter. He glimpsed rough, uneven surfaces, once more he grabbed at them in an attempt to slow himself down but the passage was growing wider and his fingers could find no hold or purchase. And then there was a sudden jolt and he was thrown upwards and landed on his stomach so that he was sliding head first now, and he saw below him a wide opening where the passage ended and beyond it he could see nothing but light and air and it was towards that hole and drop into emptiness that he was falling. Then another jolt, and a lurch, and his stomach flipped over and the passage too flipped and swung over and he was falling still but upwards now, and turning over and round like a spun coin towards the gaping and widening hole above him. He cried out and closed his eyes and folded his arms above his head, and there came a rush of air and he seemed to hang suspended for a moment before he fell down again and landed on his back on hard rock.

He felt a cold wind blowing across his face. He heard the sound of distant waves upon rocks. He breathed in and the air was sharp and made him gasp. Then he opened his eyes and he was looking up into a dull and misty grey sky.

'And now what?' said Alice.

She sat, waiting for the Voice to answer.

'Hello?' she said.

She listened. There was nothing.

'Are you there?' she said.

No answer.

Alice scratched the top of her head. She sniffed. She folded her arms then unfolded them and scratched her head again.

It was very quiet.

The last time she had heard the Voice had been just before the books had started to fall.

That part of the story had been the strangest

and most frightening of all. It had been so real. As if everything was falling down all around her. Not just the books and the stones, but the whole story. It was like when Connor kicked over her tower, only this time someone had kicked over the story and all the pieces of it were flying and falling through the air—the ship and the whale and the slimy snakes, the monsters and the things with the horrible eyes, howling sands and screaming winds and flapping wings and crashing waves. All broken to pieces and mixed up together, and she herself mixed up and falling with them. And it was then that she had heard the Voice calling out to her but as if from very far away, a long and wordless cry that faded and was lost among the tumbling and swirling pieces of story as they came crashing down to the floor.

Then she had opened her eyes and found herself sitting on the carpet in the front room among all her scattered toys and books. The fallen pieces of her tower. And there was no Voice. She realized that now. The Voice had gone and wasn't coming back.

But what about the story?

The story wasn't finished.

Usually Alice didn't worry about not finishing stories. She was always starting them and letting them go on as they wanted and then just leaving them when she couldn't think of anything else or when they just seemed to want to stop. But this story was different. She knew that this story had to be

209

finished. Because she knew that if this story didn't finish Connor wouldn't be coming back. She didn't understand how that could be, or how Connor had got himself mixed up in the story, but she knew it was something to do with the map and the broken tower, and that it was real and it was true.

But she was stuck. She didn't know how to go on with it. She couldn't say what was going to happen next. She didn't even know where they were. Her head was empty and the story lay in pieces. Scattered like the toys and books scattered across the carpet. The tower that Connor had kicked over at the beginning.

Alice had been slumped forward but now she sat up. She uncrossed her legs and stuck them straight out in front of her. Then she bent them to the side and knelt up.

At the beginning. That's where the story had started. So perhaps that was where to end it.

She listened, waiting for the Voice to tell her it was a good idea. But there was no Voice. She was on her own.

Right then.

She looked down at the book that was lying open on the floor in front of her. The book with the stories and the pictures. It was open at a picture now, a large colour picture covering a whole page, of a giant bird flying through the sky. She could tell it was a giant bird because it was holding a man in its claws. And as she looked at it she thought she heard the soft and far off whump of big wings beating. She closed the book and the sound stopped.

Better.

She moved the book aside and glanced at the toys and books scattered around her.

Which one?

That one.

She reached forward and picked up a large, red and yellow radio and cassette player made of hard plastic and placed it squarely on top of the book.

Then she looked around for something else. Another book, of nursery rhymes, a little smaller than the first book. She placed it on top of the radio.

Then she reached out and took hold of something else.

And she carried on building the tower.

He sat up. He was just below the mouth of a cave set in a craggy rock that rose some way in the air above him. A slope of scree and loose stones led down to a rocky shoreline and beyond that was the sea. A fine grey mist hung in the air, and everything was still and silent. He stood and looked up at the cave. I must have fallen right through, he thought. And come out there. Sherazhad and Sindbad too. But where were they? And where was he?

He turned away from the cave and looked down

the slope towards the shore. He wasn't far from the sealine yet it was strange that he could hear no sound of waves. Nor any other sound. And he could feel no touch of sea-breeze upon his face. And that grey mist hanging in the air so still. And the sea itself so still, motionless, and no waves moving, and no glitter of dull light off the sea's back.

He ran his eyes along the shore where the edge of the sea met the land and it was a single unbroken and unmoving line that curved away to the right and to the left at the edges of his vision. Like a pencil line drawn across paper, he thought. And remembered drawing just such a pencil line himself, when he had drawn the map. The edge of a coast, a stilled and silent sea.

It's like everything's dead, he thought. Or stopped.

The grey mist touched his skin and he shivered.

He made his way down the rockface towards the shore. The loose stones beneath his feet slid and rolled down the slope as he moved with a dull, flat rattling sound that left no after echo in the air. There was an overhang of rock to his right and as he came to the foot of the slope he saw lying beneath the overhang the bodies of Sindbad and Sherazhad.

They lay on their backs with arms outspread and legs awkwardly bent like two dolls thrown down rather than human figures. Their eyes were open and staring upwards, unblinking and unseeing. He knelt beside them. He spoke their names.

'Sherazhad? Sindbad?'

They gave no sign of hearing and did not stir. He passed his hand back and forth above their faces but there was no flicker of eye or eyelid and the gaze was fixed as if into some remote and unimaginable distance. Tentatively, he reached out a hand towards Sherazhad, and spoke her name softly again as his fingertips touched the skin of her cheek.

'Sherazhad.'

She didn't move but her skin was warm. And though her eyes didn't move there was light and life in them. Yet neither she nor Sindbad were breathing. Neither living nor dead they lay upon the rocks where they had fallen.

Connor stood. He turned and looked at the shoreline. Then he walked towards it. As he approached his footsteps began to crunch and he saw that the rock was covered in a fine, grey sand. Everything grey, he thought. No colour or life. And grey and lifeless was the sea as he stood where it touched and ran along the edge of the shore. He put out his right foot and padded the sole of his trainer on the surface of the water. It wrinkled where it was touched and then was still again.

He raised his head and looked out once more at the dull expanse of ocean and the cold mist that enshrouded it and enshrouded too the sky above it. A panic began to beat inside his stomach and his throat grew tight and suddenly he was gasping, struggling for breath as if the air around him was being sucked away. His chest was being squeezed and was starting to hurt and his eyes burned and grew blurred. But he fought against it and pushed the panic down, and gulped air deep into his lungs so that his breathing grew steadily easier and the grip on his chest relaxed. He wiped the back of his hand across his eyes to clear them and breathed in deeply a few more times until he sure he was all right. He looked once more at the shoreline, the sea, the mist. Nothing had changed. Then he turned and looked inland.

And he knew where he was, as he had known from the moment he had found himself fallen there.

A little way off was a raised, square, flat platform of rock, and the stones of the Tower of Truth were scattered upon and around it. They looked as if they had lain there for centuries. He walked away from the shore and up the slow incline until he came to the stones. They were large, square blocks with crumbling edges and corners, and had cracks in them and some had split and fallen apart into several pieces. He laid his hand upon one and ran his palm across its surface and it was dry and rough and dead. Then he put his other hand on the same surface and heaved himself up onto it and began to walk from one stone to the other until he came to the platform.

When the Tower had fallen most of its stones had been scattered around the base of the rock and only a few badly broken ones lay upon its flat surface. There was much dust there too. He stood at the centre of the platform and turned himself in a slow circle, letting his eyes gaze upon the strewn and ruined stones. And before he had completed this circle he stopped. Just a little way down from the platform there were two large stones pressed crosswise against each other, one slightly higher than the other. There was a narrow gap where their sides met and there was something pushed up out of this gap. It looked like the stem of some kind of whitish-coloured plant. He dropped down from the platform and stepped onto the first stone and squatted down to see what it was. And then he started back in horror.

It was a finger. A pale dry-skinned finger pushed up through the gap. And it had no nail.

Connor jumped to his feet, stepped backwards a few steps, then turned and ran across the stones, stumbled, twisted his foot, nearly fell, righted himself and ran off, leaping off the last stone back onto the rock and then down to the shoreline. He stood there, bent over, hands on his knees, panting, feeling the throbbing of the pain in his twisted foot. Then he straightened and turned back to look at the fallen Tower.

He's there, he thought. Trapped among the stones. And he can't escape. Trapped there for ever.

But only if the Tower stayed a ruin. If the Tower was rebuilt he would be free again, to cause what chaos and ruin he would.

He closed his eyes and in his mind saw the Tower rebuilt, saw that pale and twisted face staring out of the window. The look of triumph, of wicked intent.

He spoke aloud. 'No.'

The mist, the dull cloth of the air soaked up his voice.

And if the Tower was not rebuilt?

Then he would remain where he was, closed off from his own world for ever. And Sindbad and Sherazhad would remain trapped between life and death. And this world would be for all time what it was now, a grey, dreary, lifeless place, where nothing moved or could begin to move. And perhaps not just this world but all other worlds too.

He knew what he would have to do. The thing he was brought here for. And then he must face the consequences.

The flat sea faced him. He knelt down and bowed his head. Then he made a mark with his finger in the sand and drew the Tower.

Then there came a low humming, sensation more than sound, felt first in his finger's tip pressed into the sand, then spreading outwards, running the length of the rocky shore on which he knelt, so that it trembled beneath him, and the air about him trembled. He looked up. The sea glinted, as a ripple ran across its surface, then another, and another, and flicks and wrinkles of waves appeared, and the sea's edge crawled forward over the rocky shore, and drew back, hissing and bubbling, and reached forward again. The mist above the sea shimmered and sparkled with flecks of golden light and as he watched it melted away to reveal a clear sky above the swelling, sunlit ocean. There was a breeze sharp with the tang of ozone.

Everything's coming back to life, he thought.

A long furrowed wave washed up over the shore and around his knees. He jumped up and stepped back. The wave continued up the shore, then folded in on itself and drew back. He looked down. The drawing had gone, the sand was clear. But he knew it didn't matter. He took a breath and turned round.

The stones were no longer fallen and scattered. The Tower of Truth stood facing him. The door, the window high up. The air hummed, sang.

There was movement over to his left. He turned and Sindbad and Sherazhad were standing beneath the overhang. He laughed, then raised his hand and waved to them, calling out, and went running across the rocks towards them. They stared at him, amazed, then stepped forward to meet him with broad smiles on their faces.

'Sindbad!' he cried. 'Sherazhad! I'm so glad. It's good to see you.'

'It's good to see you,' said Sherazhad. 'We

217

thought—we didn't know what to think. Or where you were.'

'Or where we are,' said Sindbad.

'I remember falling,' said Sherazhad. 'Then— nothing. And then . . . ' She stopped, and the puzzled, dazed look came on to her face again.

'Do you know where we are?' said Sindbad.

'Yes,' said Connor. 'Look. Come on.'

He motioned them to follow him around the overhang and down to the shore. Then he pointed towards the Tower.

'We're there,' he said.

Sindbad and Sherazhad stood gazing at the Tower.

'At last,' said Sindbad.

Sherazhad turned to Connor.

'Was it you?' she said. 'Did you . . . make it? Like you made the city?'

'Yes,' said Connor.

'That was good,' she said, and smiled.

'We should go inside,' said Sindbad. 'And see what waits for us in there.'

'I think he's there,' said Connor. He didn't have to say the name. It was as if a shadow passed briefly over the sun.

Sindbad breathed out slowly.

'Then we'll we meet him again,' he said, and drew his sword from his belt and took a step towards the Tower.

But then a shadow did pass above them and there came the whoosh and thump of beaten air and a harsh, outflung cry. They looked up. Turning on wide and outspread wings as it wheeled round above the Tower, and giving out another ragged cry, a giant bird came bearing down upon them.

It was like an eagle but much bigger, with plumed head and long curved beak, and it swooped down towards them along the edge of its cry and with its legs extended and talons spread. They dropped flat to the ground and as it swept past and above them it gave a long, raucous shriek of rage. Quickly they scrambled to their feet. The bird was flying with slow and heavy wingbeats out from the island's edge and across the sea. But they could see from the way it began to tilt and turn that it was making ready for another attack.

'What is it?' said Sherazhad.

'The Rokh,' said Sindbad. 'A most fearsome bird.'

'I can see that,' said Connor.

The Rokh was wheeling round slowly above the sea. Its feathers gleamed bronze and gold in the sunlight and each feather and its plumed crest seemed tipped with dull flame.

'We'd better run,' said Sherazhad.

'To the Tower,' said Sindbad. 'Go on!'

Connor turned and ran and Sherazhad ran alongside him, the two of them racing across the rocky upward slope of the island. Connor's feet slammed and jarred against the hard surface and then the toes of one foot caught against a snag of rock and he tripped and fell. Sherazhad grabbed his hand and pulled him to his feet, and they ran on but almost immediately she too stumbled and fell. As Connor helped her up they turned and saw Sindbad some way behind them standing with sword drawn and facing upwards as the Rokh swept in, its taloned feet stretched towards him. As the bird dropped Sindbad swung his sword round and the Rokh screamed and staggered in midflight and a with a furious thrashing of its wings lurched sideways and up and turned away across the island.

Sindbad turned to face them. He was grinning.

'Abbu!' called Sherazhad. 'Come on!'

'Go on yourselves!' he called back. 'Quickly!' And he pointed up to the crag where the cave was. The giant bird was wheeling round above it, gaining height, preparing to swoop in again. Sindbad began to run towards them. 'Go on!' he cried. 'Go on!'

The bird was coming in fast.

And now they were running again and had reached the rock where the Tower stood. But before they could climb on to it there was a rush of wind and a dark shadow falling upon them and they cried out and flung their arms over their heads and dropped to their knees as the air above them was torn wide by the jag-edged scream of the bird. It passed over them, and they lowered their arms and

looked up. Then they leapt to their feet, and Sherazhad cried out.

'No!'

Sindbad was running as the Rokh swooped down
upon him. He raised his sword to strike but missed
and staggered back and the bird's talons closed
about his shoulders and lifted him off the ground.
His legs kicked at the air and as the bird rose higher
he let go his sword and reached up and wrapped his
arms around the feet that held him. His sword fell
clattering onto the rock below.

Sherazhad ran forward a few steps and raised
her head and cried out again. 'Abbu!'

Her voice seemed to leap after him but the only
reply that came back to her was a last harsh cry from
the Rokh as it beat its wings and rose higher into the
air and turned and wheeled out of sight around the
edge of the crag, and then there was silence and the
sky was empty.

She stood gazing into that blank and empty sky.
Then she lowered her head and stood like that for
some time. Connor too was looking up at the emptiness into which Sindbad had disappeared. It had
happened so suddenly he was too stunned to think
or feel anything, except a kind of dull ache inside.
Sunlight glinted off the sharp edges of the crag. The
waves hushed across the shore.

Then Sherazhad was walking back towards him and she carried the sword in her hand. She came up to him. Her eyes were shining and fierce.

'Let's go inside,' she said.

He nodded. It was like when they first met, and he was a little afraid of her again. She turned from him and placed the sword on the flat surface of the rock, then climbed on to the rock herself and picked up the sword. Connor climbed up and stood beside her.

'Are you sure he's in there?' said Sherazhad.

'I don't know,' said Connor.

'You said he was.' There was a tightness in her voice.

Connor told her what he'd seen pushed up between the stones.

'So he could be dead,' he said. 'Crushed.'

'I hope he is dead,' said Sherazhad. 'But if not . . . ' She raised the sword, then pushed its blade behind the sash at her waist and together they walked up to the door in the Tower.

It was an ordinary door of rough and unpainted wood, rounded at the top. There was no handle. Sherazhad placed her hand against the door and pushed. It creaked and swung inwards a little way. She looked at Connor and gave a half smile. Then she pushed the door fully open and went inside and Connor followed her.

They stood in a wide circular room, a little less than the circumference of the Tower. It had a low ceiling. Four narrow slits in the walls let in a little light from outside. Dust motes danced in the dim light. Opposite them a flight of three steps led up to another arched doorway. There was nothing else. Connor walked to the middle of the room and his footsteps crunched on the gritted stone floor. He stopped there and stood looking at the second door. Then he turned to Sherazhad.

'It must lead outside again,' he said.

'It can't,' said Sherazhad. 'There has to be something else in here. A way to the top at least.'

Connor shook his head, perplexed. Then he walked across to the steps and climbed them and stood in front of the doorway. Sherazhad came across and stood at the bottom of the steps.

'Open it,' she said.

He pushed the door open a little way and peered inside, then looked down at Sherazhad.

'It looks like another room,' he said.

'Let me see.'

She climbed the steps and stood beside him and pushed the door wide open. They both gasped in surprise. It was another room, circular, stone-walled like the one they were in, but about twice the size, and its ceiling much higher. It was more brightly lit too than the first, having many narrow windows in its wall. But like the first it was completely empty.

'It's impossible,' said Connor.

'Is anything impossible here?' said Sherazhad.

They went into the second room. As they made their way to the centre there came a sudden, hollow thudding sound from behind them, and they turned to see that the door they had just come through was shut. They went back to it. There was no handle and the edges of the door were flush with the frame. Connor couldn't even squeeze the tips of his fingers between them.

'I hope there's a way out of this room,' he said.

'There is,' said Sherazhad. She pointed to the left of the door. About halfway between that and the opposite side of the wall were steps leading not up this time but down. Four of them and a doorway at the bottom. They went down and pushed open the door and found themselves in another room. Again circular. But smaller than the second or first room. Dimly lit. Two steps led up on the right to another door.

So they went on, through doorway after doorway, into room after room, all circular but all of different sizes, with low or high ceilings, brightly or dimly lit, some with two or three or four or five steps leading up, some with steps leading down. Connor lost count of the number of rooms they passed through, lost all sense of direction within the Tower. He lost sense of them being inside a tower at all. It seemed more as if they had entered some vast and endless labyrinth from which there was no escape. His mind grew confused, became itself a winding and twisting labyrinth of thoughts and images, fragments of memory or dream, which when he gazed at them for too long filled him with an unaccountable horror and dread.

'Stop!'

He had cried out and hadn't known it. His voice echoed sharply around the room in which they were standing. It was narrow with high walls, illuminated only by a single shaft of light. The doorway stood at the top of four steps. Sherazhad turned to him.

'What's the matter?' she said.

'We can't go on like this,' he said. 'We're not getting anywhere.'

Sherazhad looked at him in surprise.

'But we're nearly at the top.'

'How do you know?' he said.

'I've been keeping track. There have been more steps going up than going down. So we've been getting nearer to the top. And I think we must be almost there.'

Connor hoped she was right. If they went on as they had been doing for much longer he felt he might go mad.

Sherazhad approached the steps and drew the sword from her sash.

'He might not be there,' said Connor.

'If he's not, something will be,' she said.

'Perhaps just our way home,' he said.

'Your way,' she said to him. 'Not mine.'

Connor stood with her at the bottom of the steps

which were wide enough for two to stand side by side. They climbed them together and Connor pushed the door open and they went into the next room.

It was large and brightly lit. Steps led up to a wide, high archway facing them. And in this archway, at the top of the steps, lay a dragon.

They froze.

It was an immense creature. Its head bore a single horn and gleaming tusks curved upwards from its lower jaws which rested upon its clawed feet. The long coils of its body filled the archway and spilled down the steps and across the floor in undulating waves so that the forked tip of its tail lay in the centre of the room. Its eyes were closed and it seemed to be sleeping, and its scales and horn and claws and folded wings trembled with each slow, rumbling breath. Its whole body too shimmered with different colours that swirled beneath the surface of its scaly skin, changing from red to yellow, green to violet, orange to deepest blue, as if some living jewel, lit by its own interior fires.

They stood not daring to move, hardly daring to breathe. Connor was perhaps more afraid than he had been at any other time since he had entered this world. It wasn't just the size and the appearance of the dragon, but the fact that it was resting, so that he had time to gaze fully upon it, unhindered, and with each passing moment his dread increased, and the menace enclosed within the sleeping creature's form entered more and more deeply into his mind. It seemed the very shape of his own fear.

But now Sherazhad did move. She took a single, slow step forward. But as she did the shifting colours beneath the dragon's skin swirled faster and glowed brighter and a low rumble sounded in its throat. She froze again, one foot forward, then turned to look at Connor. He shook his head. She drew her foot back. They whispered to each other.

'What shall we do?'

'I don't know.'

'We have to do something.'

'It'll wake if we go near it.'

'What, then?'

'Go back?'

Sherazhad looked back over her shoulder and her eyes started wide. She touched Connor on the arm and he turned to look. There was only wall behind them. The door through which they had come was no longer there. Connor felt like screaming. He looked at Sherazhad and saw her lips pressed tightly together, a hard and determined look on her face.

'No,' he whispered.

'There's nothing else,' she said, and shrugged, and smiled, then lifted the blade of her sword and walked towards the dragon.

It woke.

First its tail flicked and then lashed across the

floor sending a mass of swirling colours shudder-
ing the length of the creature's body. Then the great
head lifted and the eyes snapped open, each one a
blazing furnace, and the neck rose and pushed the
head forward out of the doorway, while the shimmering coils of its body unwound, and the great
beast reared up with wings stretched wide.

Sherazhad stood with sword raised, as above and
about her the creature's body hissed and crackled
with flame as if bolts of lightning flashed through its
scales and from its opened jaws a loud and terrible
thunder roared. The whole room shook and streams
of writhing colour seemed to spill out onto the floor.
Connor was pressed back against the wall, pinioned
there by the force of the blast, but Sherazhad stood
firm, and as the dragon reached its gaping jaws
towards her it seemed she held a blade of iridescent
flame in her hand that leapt up, joined with the
curling ribbons of light that flowed from the creature, and there came another roar and a blossoming
of petalled fire so bright and fierce he had to shut his
eyes against it.

When he opened them again the room was
empty. The dragon was gone. And Sherazhad was
gone too.

He stepped away from the wall. Something lay in
the centre of the room. The sword. He went over to

it and picked it up. All was silent now and still. He stood looking down at the curved blade hanging down from his hand. He thought of Sindbad who had stayed behind to strike at the giant bird and had been carried away in its talons. And he thought of Sherazhad, who had stepped forward to strike at the dragon, and now she too had been taken. He felt the heaviness of the sword drag at his arm, felt the heaviness of the stones in the wall that surrounded him. The Tower pressed down on him and he felt its weight in his heart.

Then a voice called his name. 'Connor!'

He looked up sharply. It was Sherazhad.

'Come here! Look! See what it is!'

She was calling to him from the room beyond the doorway. He walked quickly to the steps, climbed them, and went through.

She stood in the centre of the room. It was wide and high, bigger than any room they had been in yet, and from floor to ceiling its circular wall was filled with pictures. They were so bright, and so densely packed together, that his head began to swim, and he felt that he would faint and fall into their dazzle and brilliance. He shut his eyes and took a breath, then breathed out again, slowly. He felt his feet firmly planted on the floor and was standing still. He opened his eyes again.

Sherazhad was looking at him. She was smiling and her eyes shone.

'Isn't it wonderful?' she said to him.

He gazed around the wall and saw that it was made up of hundreds, perhaps thousands of square tiles and that on each tile was a different picture. Or each tile was itself a different picture. There were mountains, forests, valleys, rivers. Deserts and swamps. Cities and towns and villages. Every kind of landscape and place. And those landscapes teemed with figures of all kinds, human, animal, bird, fish. Some he recognized, some he did not. Creatures of both dream and nightmare. They shimmered and glistened and rippled with light so that they appeared almost to be moving.

He stepped closer to the wall and looked at one of the tiles and found himself staring into a wood and he could see that far back, deep among the trees was a small cottage. A hunched figure in rags stood beside the cottage and on the figure's humped shoulder sat a crow. And then it was as if he wasn't just looking into the wood, but walking into it along a path that ran through the trees, drawing nearer and nearer to the cottage, and at any moment now the crow would croak and flap its wings and the humped figure would turn and see him.

He gasped and started back.

'It's like they're real,' he said.

'I know.'

Sherazhad was standing beside him.

'But they are just pictures,' he said, and as if to

prove it to her and to himself, he raised his hand and pressed one finger against the surface of the picture. It was smooth.

'Glass,' he said. He stood back and looked around the room. 'It's all glass.'

'And the pictures are inside the glass,' said Sherazhad.

She walked over to another part of the wall and began examining some of the pictures. Connor looked at those nearest to him. In one he saw armed warriors riding out of a castle. In another a bird with golden feathers flew above a mountain top. In another a young man was singing to a serpent that was coiled around the trunk of a tree. And as he went from one to the other, Connor realized that these weren't just pictures. They were illustrations. Illustrations of stories. Each picture an episode from some strange and fantastic tale. And each time he looked at one, the same happened as with the first. It was as if he was entering that story, walking into its world, and it was about to come to life around him.

And he could not only see the stories, he could hear them. That humming sound. It was coming from here, from this room. From all these pictures, these stories. Like the buzzing of thousands of bees in a hive. And like them, each story a living creature.

Some words of Trismagistus's came back to him, half-recalled.

The Tower at the centre. Holding everything together.

Holding all these stories and making them live.

Then something made him start and his heart thump. He was staring at a picture and suddenly he realized what it was he was seeing. He blinked and shook his head and looked again to make sure he wasn't mistaken. No. It was there before him. A giant bird with a great hooked beak and huge talons extended down from its body as it flew. And there was a man hanging from its talons. Connor recognized the bird and he recognized the man. The bird was the Rokh and the man was Sindbad.

But that wasn't all. The picture next to that one was of Sindbad as well, this time standing on a high cliff looking down into a valley filled with snakes and jewels. And next to that Sindbad with an old man sitting on his shoulders, legs wrapped around Sindbad's neck. And next to that Sindbad on a ship in the middle of a storm. Connor remembered overhearing Sindbad in the desert that night telling Sherazhad about the adventures he'd had. And here they were. And there he was, back in his stories. Back in his world.

And while he was still gazing in astonishment at the pictures, Sherazhad called out to him.

'Come here! Look at this! Look!' There was such an urgency and excitement in her voice that Connor went running across to where she was standing, pointing at one of the pictures. It was even more astonishing than those he'd just seen.

'Do you see?' said Sherazhad.

Connor nodded. He couldn't speak.

'It's me,' she said.

There was a man sitting on a throne, dressed in fine robes. He looked like a king. Others sat on either side of him on large cushions. All were leaning forward, an intent look on their faces. They were looking at a figure sitting before them on the floor, one arm raised, a finger lifted. She was speaking to them and they were listening, absorbed by what they heard. Though her face was in profile, and she was wearing a red and richly embroidered dress, he could see that it was Sherazhad.

'I'm a telling a story.' He heard her voice speaking close to him. 'And my name isn't Sherazhad. It's Shaharazad. I'm a storyteller. Every night I tell a new story. And all listen to me, and are filled with the wonder and enchantment of my tales.'

He looked away from the girl in the picture, looked at the same girl standing beside him.

'You remember,' he said.

'Yes,' she said. 'I remember.' She was still gazing at the picture, and raised her hand now and pressed her fingers to the glass. Then drew them back sharply, and gave a gasp. Ripples were spreading across the glass where she had touched it as if she had placed her fingers against the surface of a

233

pool of water. They watched as the picture wrinkled and shivered and then the ripples faded and it was still once more. Then they looked at each other, and Sherazhad smiled with delight. Her hand was still raised and her fingers were trembling. She touched them against the glass once more, and once more its surface rippled and this time she let her fingers sink into those ripples, so that the picture seemed to melt. And then the ripples were running along her hand, and her arm, and across her body, so that she seemed no longer a figure of flesh and blood but a shimmering image lying at the bottom of some deep pool, and she and the picture were dissolving into each other.

Her voice spoke to him as if from far off, at the bottom of that deep pool.

'I'm going there,' she said. 'Back to my story. Back home. Goodbye. I won't forget you. And I won't forget this story. Goodbye . . . '

Her final words faded away as her body melted and faded and the ripples that ran across the picture slowed and settled and stilled and he was looking at Sherazhad—or Shaharazad—telling her story as her audience listened, entranced. But she no longer stood beside him. She was back in her world, where she belonged.

'Goodbye,' he said.

But where was his world, his story? Surely that too must be here somewhere. He had to find it and get back to it. Back home.

'It's here.'

His body stiffened. The voice was cold and thin, an icy whisper, and he had been expecting to hear it ever since he had entered the Tower. He still held the sword in his hand and his grip upon it tightened. Then he took a breath and turned to face Trismagistus.

His hood was pulled back to reveal the pale, dry-skinned face, the skin stretched tight across the hairless dome of his head, the eyes gazing from their dark sockets. He stepped from the doorway into the room. He spoke softly, a hoarse, grating whisper.

'You thought I was dead. Crushed beneath the stones of the Tower.' He came forward a few more steps. 'I was. But I have been dead before and risen again.'

He now walked to the middle of the room and stood there, gazing round at the wall filled with pictures.

The humming grew louder.

'A thousand lives,' he said. 'A thousand deaths. And a thousand lives lived again. Over and over. A thousand and one.' He laughed, harsh and bitter. Then stopped abruptly, and when he spoke again there was a sigh of sadness in that whispered voice, a melancholy glimmer in his eyes' cold light. 'I have been them all. All of these stories, and many more. Sometimes one character, sometimes another. I have fought with monsters, and I have been those monsters. I have seen marvels and wonders, horrors and terrors. I have crossed timeless lands and endless, rolling oceans. World after world after world.' He looked at Connor. 'Do you understand?'

'I'm not sure,' said Connor. He was trying to concentrate on what Trismagistus was saying, but that humming, buzzing sound was getting in the way, like some electrical interference.

Trismagistus smiled, thin-lipped.

'In the beginning I was like you. Confused, lost. Afraid. Then I forgot my confusion and my fear. I relished the adventure, took delight in the thrills, the danger, the excitement. I flung myself joyfully into each fresh encounter. Endless lives to be lived, endless stories in which to play. Oh, the utter joy and freedom of it!' He came forward, stood in front of Connor, laid a white, bony hand upon his shoulder. 'But then slowly,' he said, 'very slowly, I began to understand. To see the truth of it. The truth that was a lie. A deception. The Tower of Truth? The Tower of Lies! Not endless freedom! A prison. Trapped here in these stories, these lies. And no way out of them, unless I could break free. Find a way out, a way of escape. That's what I've been searching for. And now at last I've found it.' His voice dropped to the softest, grating whisper. 'We shall escape from here

236

together.'

He brought his face close to Connor's, fixed him with his cold and glittering eyes. He was waiting for Connor to say something. But what could he say? Trismagistus's words whirled inside his head and he was trying hard to catch hold of them, make some sense of them. But could he trust them? Could he believe anything Trismagistus told him? He tried to think, to clear his mind, but that humming sound, that deep electrical drone was breaking up his thoughts and flinging them away from him.

Trismagistus's fingers pressed harder into his shoulder.

'If not you will become as I am now. And we will both be lost for ever.'

And out of the sharp pain caused by Trismagistus's grip, Connor found his voice to speak.

'You abandoned us,' he said. 'In the chamber. It was falling down around us and you left us there.'

The cold flames in his eyes flickered, flared.

'And you crushed me beneath the stones of the Tower,' he said. 'And so we're quits.' His fingers pressed harder, deeper into Connor's shoulder, and Connor felt all strength, all will, beginning to drain from him. And all he wanted was to be free of that grip, to be out of this nightmare, back where he was safe again.

'I just want to go home,' he said.

Trismagistus loosed his grip.

'You still don't see, do you?' said Trismagistus. 'Or you won't see. There is no home, no world for you to go back to. This is your world.' He let go of Connor's shoulder, stepped back, swept his arm around the circle of glittering, living pictures. 'All these worlds, these stories. They are endless, and you will live in them for ever, as I have. What I am, you will become. Unless you break free of them. Destroy them.'

Connor shook his head, tried to rid himself of that humming, buzzing interference, shouted through it to make himself heard.

'Destroy the Tower? What do you mean? What are you talking about? You said I had to build it again. And I've done that. So why can't I go back? Tell me!'

The humming grew louder still, and there was the high-pitched whine now too, a sharp wire drawn clean through the centre of the drone. Drawn through the centre of Connor's skull.

Trismagistus raised both his arms, spread them wide.

'Not the Tower. A thing of stone that can fall and rise again. The Tower is a mask. It is the thing behind that mask you must destroy.'

He began to pace around the room. Connor tried to keep his eyes on him, but he was moving too quickly and the light that shone from or through the glass pictures on the wall played in varicoloured shafts and streams across him as he moved. His robe flapped about him and seemed edged with rainbow flickerings of flame. His words flew about the room, wild, crazed, as difficult to catch hold of as his shifting form.

'The thing that creates and controls all. That hidden, infernal power. Maker of worlds and tales, each tale a world, each world a story never ending. That cruel tyrant that brought me here, and holds me fast against my will. And will hold you unless you strike.'

He stood once more in the centre of the room, facing towards Connor, and he seemed filled with colour and light, the images on the walls projected onto his body, as if they now moved and lived in him. Connor stared at him, transfixed. The wire was pulling tighter through his head, a bright and piercing scream, and the room howled and Trismagistus's voice howled with it.

'Strike. Raise the sword. Strike through the mask and set us free!'

And now it seemed to Connor that he stood outside himself, watching himself, as if watching the enactment of some ancient tale. Saw how he gripped the sword's hilt with both hands, and lifted its blade high above his head, and turned to face the wall, and prepared to bring it crashing down upon its painted mirrored surface. But what would happen to all those stories if he did? What would become of Sindbad and Sherazhad? Would they and their worlds be destroyed for ever? Perhaps the way back to his own world was through destroying theirs.

'Strike!'

Trismagistus cried aloud and his cry was one with the roar and scream of the Tower.

'Strike!'

And the pictures before Connor's eyes blurred, melted. Their colours swirled and fractured and re-formed, and became not many but one, a single image multiplied a thousand times. From every mirrored surface the face of Trismagistus stared at him.

'Strike!'

The screaming wire inside him snapped. His body jerked. He struck.

And every mirrored surface shivered, split and burst into fragments. They flew outwards, glittering shards of glass and light and sound swirling around the room. Connor dropped the sword, fell back, saw Trismagistus at the centre of that screeching storm, caught in a blaze of white light that itself then cracked and splintered and flew into fragments with the rest, whirled and spun to fine silver threads which crumbled into powdered dust that hung a moment, drifting in the air, then dissolved and was gone.

And all was silence then, and Connor stood alone in the empty, stone-walled room.

EIGHT
The New World

He stood, listening. There was no sound. The room was bare, empty. Stone, circular wall, stone ceiling, stone floor. A single arched window let in light from outside.

He examined his arms, his hands, his legs, ran his fingers over his face, looking for signs of injury, small cuts, but there were none. The flying glass had left him untouched, unharmed. The sword lay on the floor where it had fallen. Its blade was broken in two.

He walked over to the window and looked out. There was the rocky shoreline, the sea beyond. He stood away, turned. The doorway stood on the far side of the room, arched, like the window. He walked towards it. Then he went through.

It didn't lead to another room but to a short, narrow passage. At the end of the passage was a mirror. He walked up to it and stood in front of it.

The mirror was empty. No reflection. The glass a blank face.

He waited.

The mirror began to cloud. It filled with a smokiness that grew thicker, and then he saw something hidden behind the smokiness, something he couldn't quite make out. He stood watching. The smokiness drifted, thinned, and what was hidden became clearer, and clearer still. Until the smokiness was gone and he was looking at what lay within the mirror.

It was his living room at home. There was the table, with sheets of paper on it, the window behind the table. His sister sat on the carpet. In front of her was a tower made of toys and books. Her hand was raised in the act of placing a small wooden block on top of the tower. But all was stilled, frozen. The story stopped, waiting to continue. Waiting for him.

He stepped forward into and through the mirror. Into his story.

Alice placed the wooden block on top of the tower then carefully took her hand away. She sat back and looked at it. It was a good tower and she was very pleased with it. And with herself. She looked up.

'Hello, Connor,' she said.

'Hello, Alice,' he said.

'I've made the tower again,' she said.

'I can see.' He walked over to the tower, crouched down in front of it, on the other side from Alice.

'It's good,' he said.

'I know.'

'I'm sorry for kicking the other one over.'

She shrugged.

'That's all right. This one's better.'

'It is,' he said.

Alice wrinkled her nose and rubbed it with the back of her hand.

'I shouldn't have scribbled on your drawing,' she said.

'That's OK,' he said. 'I can put it right.'

She looked at him and seemed about to say something, but she didn't, so he stood up and went to the table and looked at the map. The Tower stood on its island. It wasn't scribbled over. There was no face looking out of the window. He touched it and felt a tingling in the ends of his fingers.

Alice sat looking at her tower. She thought about her story and started telling Connor about it.

'I've been making up a story,' she said. 'It was very strange and very exciting. A lot of weird things happened. There was a ship in a storm, and a whale, and monsters in a desert, and a big shiny city. And there were two pirates in it, and the man with the horrible face that I saw in the tower. And you were in it as well.'

She looked away from her tower towards the table. Connor was standing there looking at her.

'I didn't make it up all by myself,' she said. 'There was a voice helping me. Sometimes I made things happen and sometimes the voice made things happen. And sometimes we made things happen together.'

'What kind of voice?' said Connor.

'I don't know,' said Alice. 'Just a voice. It's gone now.' Then she looked hard at Connor and narrowed her eyes. 'Do you believe me?' she said to him.

'Yes,' he said. 'I believe you.'

She seemed relieved.

'Some of it was very frightening,' she said.

'It was,' said Connor. 'But everything turned out all right in the end.'

'Everything turned out as it should,' said Alice.

Connor stood at the table. He listened. There was a humming noise. The sound of the vacuum cleaner from upstairs.

'Has Mom been down?' he said.

'Once,' said Alice. 'She asked me where you were and I said I didn't know.' She cocked her head to one side. 'Where were you?' she said.

'In your story,' said Connor.

He grinned. Then Alice grinned. And then she took the wooden block from the top of her tower.

'What are you doing?' he said.

'I'm starting again,' she said.

Then she took off the next piece and the next, and placed them on the floor beside her.

'Good idea,' he said.

He sat at the table and looked at his map. Then he picked up his pencil.

And then he was standing in front of the mirror,

watching Alice take the pieces from her tower, watching himself bent over the table, drawing. His throat tightened and there came a moment of panic when his mind became fogged and he didn't know which was real, the image in the mirror, or himself, standing here, looking at the image in the mirror. The floor seemed to slip from under him and the whole tower was toppling sideways and he was falling with it into nothingness. Then suddenly all was steady and solid again and once more he was looking at himself in the mirror, in the other world. A voice spoke in his head.

They're both real. You there, and you here. Two lives being lived, two stories being told. And both at the same time.

He spoke in his head to the voice.

How can that be? In two places at once? I don't understand.

The Voice replied.

It doesn't matter if you don't understand. Not straightaway. Many things are unknown, only dimly glimpsed. Understanding of them comes slowly, as you go on with your journey.

My journey, he said. Where?

Wherever your path takes you. That too is unknown until you take it.

He glanced into the mirror where he sat at the table drawing, where Alice was sitting on the floor with her books and her toys. He saw her lips moving, speaking softly to herself.

Like one of my sister's stories, he said.

Like one of your sister's stories, said the Voice.

And though he could not see who or what was speaking, and did not know from where the voice came, he thought there was traced upon it the warmth of a smile.

He spoke again. He was still looking in the mirror.

Can I go back there?

You are already there. Your life goes on as it did.

I mean like before, when I went through the mirror.

Of course.

What will happen if I do?

You will be there. And you will not return here.

Once more he felt a tremor of panic.

What about later? Can I ever go back?

The road you take will return here. Unless you become lost.

He thought about that for a while. Then he said, Like Trismagistus.

Like he who was Trismagistus, said the Voice. And he is lost for ever.

And now there was something he understood. He was being offered this one chance, this gift, and if he took it, it was up to him what he made of it.

The Voice spoke again, and it was the last time it spoke.

Everything is a story. And all stories are one. And

they begin here, and begin now.

Then there arose in his mind a vision of vast land-scapes and distances, of deep skies lit and horizons of blurred shadow, and paths for the taking running through them, and he alone upon those paths, and his tread upon them free and unconstrained. But even at the same time he raised his hand towards the mirror, where he was living still his other life, unconscious of this one, and made as if to press his fingers against its smooth and pliant surface. But he did not touch the glass, and his hand remained for a moment lifted in a seeming gesture of farewell. The mirror shivered, and the image it held, and a smoki-ness filled the room, the glass, obscuring all that lay behind it. Then the smokiness cleared and the mir-ror was empty.

He lowered his hand. It was time to go.

He turned from the mirror and walked back along the passageway. There was no doorway at the end, but some steps that led downwards, winding around a stone column. He went down the steps, to the bottom. Facing him, in the circular stone wall, there was a wooden door. It was closed, but from underneath he could see a pale light coming in from outside.

He became aware of a faint humming, a deep drone that trembled in the stones of the Tower.

He put his hand on the latch and lifted it, and pulled the door open and stepped out. He walked away from the Tower down to the shore. The waves washed over the bare rock, bubbles of white foam, hiss and whisper. A wind stirred. He looked out across the ocean. There was a mistiness on the horizon that glimmered with pale light, and through the mistiness he could make out the faint, hazy outline of ragged cliffs rising high into the sky.

'The northern lands,' he said.

He watched them. From the shadows of those clifftops something dark rose into the air, thickened, lengthened, began to take on shape and form as it drew nearer across the ocean. Whether creature or craft he couldn't tell, some visitant from the world's edge. The light flickered and darted around it, and soon it would be near enough for him to see what it was.

Connor stood, waiting.

Something was happening and he was ready for it.

David Calcutt is a novelist, playwright, and poet. As a boy, he liked reading comics, going to the cinema, and acting out stories he had made up.
Among the books that fired his imagination were Treasure Island, Moby Dick, and Beowulf, and these remain favourites. Mythology, folklore, and archaeology are other sources of inspiration.

David has three children and he and his wife live in the Midlands.